# The Four Towers

by Kerry Marie Sloan

STARGAZER BOOKS
*Philadelphia*

# STARGAZER
## BOOKS

This STARGAZER BOOKS paperback edition July 2019

STARGAZER BOOKS and the STARGAZER BOOKS logo are trademarks of STARGAZER BOOKS LLC.

For information about special discounts for bulk purchases, book signings, and talks by the author please contact

Special Events - Stargazer Books
info@stargazerbooks.com
or visit our website
www.stargazerbooks.com

*Design by Dan Yager*

Manufactured in the United States of America

Library of Congress Control Number: 2019944460

ISBN-13: 978-1-944523-08-4
ISBN-10: 1-944523-08-1

To Annmarie.

# CONTENTS

# PROLOGUE
# CAROLINE

aroline's breath came in ragged gasps. The object was far heavier than she had expected. She rested against the rough-hewn stones of the parapet wall for a moment to catch her breath, shivering as she peered ahead into the gloom. It was a chilly night and the fog was coming in, enshrouding the castle walls. She knew she didn't have much time. Her husband was sure to notice her thievery, and when he did, he would pursue her.

Caroline adjusted her hold on the object and began running again. Her bare feet were scraped and torn from the rough surfaces of the castle. Her nightgown billowed in the wind and her golden hair whipped around her face in a disordered, tangled mess.

Caroline thought again of her once beloved husband, Edward. How had he become a creature to be feared? It was only a few years ago that they had married. Caroline had never experienced such happiness. But then something had changed. Edward started spending long nights in his study, poring over ancient books and manuscripts. He obsessed over frightening, foul smelling experiments. Caroline tried to talk to him, tried to entice him away from his new pursuits, but to no avail. He was a different man.

Caroline paused again to catch her breath, and it was then that she saw it. She froze as she gazed at the sight in horror.

Caroline had never really believed the strange tales and rumors. It was all too fantastic to be true. But there it was, looming eerily in the darkness ahead of her, the Fourth Tower. She could only make out a vague outline. The tower itself was almost transparent. But there was no denying that it was there.

The Montclairs, her husband's family had lived in the castle for hundreds of years. They had built three towers around its perimeter, and there had been plans to build a fourth. But it had never been completed. Caroline had always found a strange sense of romance in the unfinished end of the building. She had laughed at the rumors of a strange shadowy tower that people claimed they could see from time to time. How could anyone see something that wasn't there?

But then, Edward had started talking about the tower too. She hadn't understood him at the time, but she thought she did now. The tower was a part of his evil pursuits. It was there that the stone had to be destroyed.

Caroline heard a sound behind her and she stopped short in fear. It was Edward! It had to be! She could hear him, muttering and cursing. He sounded like the devil himself! He was gaining on her. She was so tired, and the stone was so heavy, and it only seemed to be getting heavier. How was she going to make it to the tower?

Caroline willed her exhausted body onward. She was no longer running, but walking in long, painful strides. As she neared the tower, she paused, gazing at the sight before her in dread. The shadowy gray tower terrified her. She had no desire to go any further. But there was no choice. Her husband was almost upon her. She could hear him clearly now. She almost fell, but righted herself just in time, scraping her arm and ripping her nightgown on the castle wall.

Caroline forced herself to place one foot onto the shadowy parapet of the fourth tower. To her surprise, her foot met solid ground. She inched forward slowly, still unsure that the shimmery, unreal edifice would hold her. But it did. Gathering all of her remaining courage, she rushed forward, across the top of the tower to the interior stairs of the structure.

Before she had descended more than a few stairs, she heard her husband above her.

"Caroline," he snarled, peering through the swirling shadows. "Give me back what is rightfully mine."

Caroline's eyes filled with tears as she gazed at the man she had once loved. She couldn't reply, but only shook her head sorrowfully.

"The choice isn't yours!" he said, wildly. "The stone is mine!"

As he spoke, he waved his arms and the tower floor below Caroline roared to life, a fiery pit was directly below her, the flames licking at the stairs.

"I will destroy you!" he shouted.

Caroline took one last long look at her husband. "No," she whispered. "I will destroy it."

She took a shivering breath and leaped forward into the flames, holding the stone before her.

"No!" shouted Edward, and, with an anguished cry, he plunged into the flames after her.

# CHAPTER I
# LONDON

arah stood on the bridge looking into the dark river below. It was early evening and the light was slowly fading around her. The sky was a deep blue color and a few stars were just barely visible. It was Sarah's favorite time of day, and she looked around her with a contented sigh. Her week in London had been lovely, and she was reluctant to leave. But it was time. She was due to join Molly in the countryside for a two-week summer vacation.

"Thank you Uncle Alfred," she whispered to herself. The London trip had been his idea. And it had been wonderful! It was her first time in the city and she had loved every minute of it. And it was a trip that she needed. Sarah hadn't realized how exhausted she was until she arrived in London.

So much had happened to her in such a short space of time! Sarah had started attending Westmere Academy the previous fall as a transfer student. The students at the exclusive Westmere did not look kindly on outsiders, and Sarah had struggled. To make matters worse, Sarah wasn't an ordinary student. She was different, part of a secret order called the Guardians. While Sarah was at Westmere, her powers had been tested to their limit by an ancient evil residing in a manuscript called the Book of Westmere. She had triumphed and made several close friends in the process. But the experience had been very hard on her.

Sarah pushed back her dark hair and sighed. There was still so much to think about and so much to decide. She had graduated from Westmere in the spring. Her uncle had told her that she could begin her duties as a Guardian immediately, or that she could take some time off to further her education. She didn't know what to do. She knew there were still many perils ahead of her....her parents for one thing. But she was so tired. She didn't know if she could face another challenge like the Book of Westmere without a chance to rest first.

Sarah's reverie was broken by the clock striking the hour. She looked up at the imposing facade of Parliament and Big Ben. If she didn't hurry, she was going to miss her train. Sarah looked around again, attempting to fix everything in her memory. She didn't want to forget any of the incredible things she had experienced in the city.

Sarah crossed the Thames and walked briskly down the road towards the Waterloo train station. Her train was due to leave in about forty-five minutes. She had just enough time to get to the station and do a little exploring along the way. Sarah ducked down a side street and then another. She wanted to enjoy her last moments wandering about the city.

Sarah was feeling quite happy and content with her walk, but after a few moments, she noticed a change. She couldn't put her finger on what it was at first. It had grown very quiet, but that was to be expected since she was no longer on a main thoroughfare. But for some time, she hadn't seen any other pedestrians or any vehicles driving by. The streets she was taking weren't well traveled, but they shouldn't be deserted. It had also grown very dark, too dark for the time of day. It was early evening, not the middle of the night.

Sarah tried not to get nervous, but she could feel the tension rising.

"You're just imagining things," she said to herself. "It's nothing but your nerves!"

Despite these reassurances, Sarah did not feel calm. She looked around, attempting to find a way back to the main road. Why had she ever taken these narrow, winding streets? It seemed like a very bad idea.

Something was definitely wrong. There was no denying it now. All of her instincts as a Guardian were warning her. She could feel the evil in the air. She looked down at the small gold ring that she wore on her left hand. It was pulsing faintly. In the past, it had served as a warning sign when she was in danger. Was that what it was trying to tell her now?

But why here and now? She was in England on a vacation; she wasn't pursuing an assignment. It didn't make any sense. But perhaps it was something else. Could someone be following her? Was that was what she was sensing?

Sarah paused in her rapid strides and looked around anxiously. If someone was following her she wanted to know who and why. But there were still no signs of life. No people, no cars, no lights in the houses around her. It was eerie and Sarah shuddered in fear.

Despite herself, Sarah broke into a run. She couldn't help it. The air was getting thick around her and it was difficult to breathe normally. She could feel more intensely now the darkness behind her. She was running as fast as she could, but it was still overtaking her. Either she got away or she would have to turn around and face her pursuer. And, right now, she wasn't sure she had the strength to fight a powerful opponent.

Before Sarah could decide what to do, her foot hit an uneven stretch of pavement and she lost her balance. As she fell, she whispered a few words of protection. There was nothing else she could do. They were all she had. She only hoped they would work.

*****

Sarah sensed vaguely the figure of someone bending over her. She didn't know where she was for a moment, and then she suddenly remembered it all....the evil pursuing her, the fear, and the horrible danger.

She started up, ready to protect herself from whatever horror she now faced.

"Hey, be careful there," laughed a familiar voice.

"Arthur!" said Sarah, completely shocked. Arthur was the last person she had expected to see.

Sarah had met Arthur at Westmere Academy. At first, the two had been enemies, but then, incredibly, they realized that Arthur also had the gifts of a Guardian. During their time at Westmere together, Arthur had developed his own powers and been taken into the group. He had helped Sarah defeat the evil at Westmere. And, in the process, he had become a close friend and ally.

"What are you doing here?" she asked. "I thought you weren't due in England for another few days!"

"I wasn't," replied Arthur, with a smile. "But I was able to get away earlier than I thought from your uncle. He can be a real slave driver sometimes, but he decided to give me a break from Guardian History 101 so I could surprise you in London. He told me what train you were planning on taking and I figured I'd join you."

"But I didn't expect to find you like this!" he continued. "Are you okay?" he asked, offering a helping hand to pull her up.

"I think so," said Sarah, still a bit dazed by everything that had happened.

"How did you find me?" she asked.

"Now that's an incredible coincidence!" said Arthur. "I wasn't sure which way you'd be coming, so I figured I'd just meet you at the train. But after I got to the station, I decided to walk around a little. I turned down this side street, and when I did, you were right in front of me. I wasn't expecting to find you on the ground, but at least I found you!"

Sarah tried to smile. "I guess I'm not known for my grace," she said ruefully, as she rubbed a bruised elbow.

"You're not hurt, are you?" asked Arthur, with a look of concern.

"No," said Sarah. "Maybe just a little embarrassed."

"Nothing to be embarrassed about," said Arthur, taking her by the arm. "These streets are very uneven....the best of us fall from time to time."

"But why were you running?" he asked, curiously. "When I turned the corner, I saw you running down the road, as if someone was chasing you."

Sarah looked away, wondering if she should tell Arthur what had happened. Maybe she had imagined the whole thing? She didn't want to cause any unnecessary alarm. And everything looked so normal now. There were lights on in the houses and businesses lining the street. The normal city noises were all around them. There were people walking about and cars driving by.

Maybe there hadn't been anyone following her, maybe it was just her mind playing tricks on her. Arthur hadn't noticed anything odd either. If there had been something evil pursuing her, he would have felt it too, wouldn't he?

"I was afraid I was going to miss the train," said Sarah, hoping Arthur wouldn't notice her face reddening. She hated to lie, but she wasn't sure that she had anything to tell. A strange feeling? An imagined presence? No, it was better this way.

"Don't worry about that...we're early," said Arthur. "We have more than enough time for you to tell me all about London before we get on the train. And I'm sure you want to hear about your uncle and all of the fun we've had together. How does that sound?"

"That sounds wonderful," said Sarah, beginning to feel a bit better. Arthur's unexpected presence was making everything seem normal again.

"Everything will be okay....I hope," she whispered to herself.

# CHAPTER II
# COUNTRY

 arah awoke to the sun streaming through her
bedroom window. She sighed contentedly and
slowly opened her eyes. She was in a small room
on the third floor of the farmhouse owned by
Molly's aunt and uncle. She had arrived late the previous
evening and had gone straight to bed, barely making it
through the introductions to Molly's family.

Sarah looked around her room curiously. It was small but
cozy. A narrow, multi-paned window looked out onto the
fields bordering the house and the hills beyond. The bed,
covered with a thick, hand-stitched quilt, was nestled into a
small alcove where the slanting ceiling met the wall. There was
a tiny, white table next to the bed and an antique wooden
dresser in the corner topped with a vase of colorful
wildflowers.

Suddenly, a small frown creased Sarah's brow. She had just
remembered something unpleasant...a nightmare from the
previous evening. In her dream, she had been in London and
someone had been chasing her. Sarah shuddered as she
thought about it. But it hadn't been a dream, it had really
happened! Or had it? It was all so vague now. All she could
remember clearly was her own fear and a deep sense of danger,
but had it been real or had she only imagined it?

Hoping to distract herself, Sarah pulled herself out of bed

and went to the window. She opened the it a crack to let in the crisp morning air. It was still cool outside, although the day promised to be warm. She could just make out two men in the distance coming down from the hills, a large flock of sheep trailing behind them. Sarah smiled. She had forgotten that Molly's uncle kept sheep. It was a lovely sight.

Pushing her unpleasant thoughts aside, Sarah said to herself, "I'm here to rest and enjoy myself, and that's exactly what I intend to do."

*****

Sarah descended the steep stairs leading from the third floor. She could hear voices coming from the center of the house. The house was old and large and had lots of small rooms and narrow hallways, but Sarah was still able to find the kitchen without too much trouble.

When Sarah entered the room, Molly and a woman in her late forties were sitting at the table laughing.

"Sarah!" said Molly, with pleasure. "I'm so glad you're awake. We've been talking about you."

"I hope I wasn't rude last night," said Sarah, as she extended her hand in greeting. "I was so tired all I could think about was going to bed."

"Of course not," replied Molly's aunt, taking Sarah warmly by the hand. "Traveling can be exhausting."

"Sarah," said Molly, in an official tone of voice, "this is my aunt Caroline Collicott."

"It's so nice to meet you," said Sarah, with a smile. "Molly's told me so much about you."

"And we've heard so much about you," replied Caroline. "I think Molly's had more excitement in her life since she met you than any of us will ever have!"

Sarah reddened slightly, thinking about The Book of Westmere. Molly had played a role in the events that took place at Westmere, but she didn't know the truth about Sarah and the Guardians.

"Molly thinks I'm much more exciting than I really am," said Sarah, trying to change the subject. "I'm actually very boring."

"Well," replied Caroline, "I hope the two of you aren't bored here this summer. Besides the sheep and the countryside, there isn't much for two young girls to do."

"I don't think there's any danger of us being bored," said Sarah. "In fact, I'm looking forward to a very quiet visit. It will be a nice change."

"And the countryside around here is so beautiful," said Molly. "I can't wait to show you some of my favorite places."

"Plus you have your boys in town for a few weeks. And I think Molly mentioned another friend coming to visit for a little while too," said Caroline.

"Right," answered Molly. "Arthur and Daniel are staying in the village. And we might get to see Margaret, at least for a few days."

"Margaret!" said Sarah, in surprise. "I thought that she was too busy! Isn't she in Paris for the whole summer?"

"She is," said Molly, "She's working at one of her father's companies. But she has to come to London for work. She might try to visit us during her trip."

Sarah smiled, thinking about how strange it was that Margaret would want to come see her and Molly. It was still a bit odd to think of her as a friend. When Sarah had started at Westmere Academy, Margaret had been her chief persecutor. Things had certainly changed a lot in a few months!

Just then, there was a bustle at the door and a large, burly man entered, clearly Molly's uncle. He was followed reluctantly by a thin, dark-haired young man.

"Uncle Jacob!" said Molly with delight. "We missed you this morning!"

"Sorry dear," he smiled at his niece. "We were up well before the sun. It's not everyone who has the luxury to sleep all day."

"Don't be silly, Uncle," laughed Molly. "You know I don't sleep all day."

"But you have to meet Sarah," continued Molly. "She was half asleep when she arrived last night. I don't think she even remembers talking to you."

Jacob grasped Sarah's hand. "We're so happy to have you here with us."

"Thank you," said Sarah. "I'm very happy to be here, and I know I'm going to enjoy it."

"And this is Jordan," said Molly, gesturing towards the dark figure who was hovering behind Jacob in the shadow of the door. "He's here for the summer to help on the farm."

Jordan looked up at Sarah and nodded. His eyes were a very dark blue and contrasted sharply with his dark hair and pale skin.

Sarah returned his nod slowly. There was something about his face that seemed vaguely familiar. She was sure they'd never met before. But he reminded her of someone.

"He doesn't talk that much but he's the best hand I've ever had on the farm," said Jacob. "I've never seen animals take to someone like they do with Jordan. He has the gift."

Jacob put his hand affectionately on Jordan's shoulder. "I gave him the day off yesterday and I thought things were going to fall apart," he continued. "I don't know what I'm going to do when he leaves at the end of the summer."

Jordan reddened and then slipped quickly from the room. "I have some work to do in the barn," he muttered.

"You should have asked him to stay," said Caroline, looking regretfully after Jordan's retreating figure.

"Do you think that would have made a difference?" asked Jacob. "He's shy."

"I know," said Caroline, "he just seems so lonely."

"He'll be alright. He just needs a little more time to get used to us," answered Jacob. "But right now, we have more important things to think about. What's for breakfast?"

"You already had breakfast this morning before you left,"

answered Caroline.

"That was hours ago," replied Jacob, with a smile. "I'm hungry again!"

"We were just about to make something special in honor of Sarah's arrival," said Molly.

"Well you better make lots of it, because I'm starving," he said.

"And," Jacob continued, with a playful glance at Sarah. "I want to hear all about you and Molly and everything you've been up to over the past few months. Molly's told us some tremendous stories! And even more importantly, you have to tell us about this young beau that Molly's got stashed up in town. We haven't met him yet and I'm not sure that we approve."

"Uncle Jacob," said Molly, reddening. "Daniel only just got here. I don't see how you could have met him already."

"Well," said Jacob, with a wink at Sarah, "I don't know anything about this boy and as Molly's uncle I think I should have some say in her choice of associates."

Sarah laughed. "I don't think you have anything to worry about. Daniel's about as perfect a boyfriend as anyone could want. They make a nice couple."

Molly's blush deepened. "If this is how we're going to spend the morning, then I think I'll go to my room."

"Now don't you worry, dear," laughed Jacob. "I won't keep picking on you. I have Sarah to think about too. We haven't even started to talk about her boyfriend."

Sarah laughed again. "I don't have one. And if you're thinking of Arthur he's certainly not my boyfriend! He's more like my brother."

"Then it's our job to find you one," said Jacob slyly. "Now," he said, addressing himself to Caroline, "who do you think we can find in the village for Sarah? What about the oldest Brompton boy? He seems like he might be a good catch."

"Jacob," replied Caroline. "You're worse than a matchmaker! They're here to enjoy themselves. Not to find husbands!"

"Well," said Jacob, grabbing his wife playfully by the hand, "a husband isn't a bad thing to have, is it?"

"I don't know," laughed Caroline, as she disentangled herself. "Some days I'm not that sure."

*****

"I'd like to take Sarah to the Four Towers this afternoon," said Molly to her aunt, as she helped clear up the dishes from the breakfast feast they had just finished. "Do you think Uncle Jacob would want to come with us?"

Caroline looked at Molly and grimaced, "What do you think?" she said.

"Is he really still so dead set against the place?" asked Molly.

"You know Jacob," said Caroline. "He doesn't believe in any of the old stories. He's perfectly logical and rational about everything. Plus he's not from the village originally. Maybe it's just not in his blood."

"What are you talking about?" asked Sarah, curiously. She had left the room for a moment to wash up, but returned in time to hear the end of Caroline's answer to Molly.

"Oh goodness," said Caroline, with a smile, "we're getting our guest involved in a family controversy already."

Sarah looked at Caroline with interest. "You're making me even more curious," she said.

"If anyone would be interested in the Four Towers it would be Sarah," said Molly, eagerly. "In fact, she might be able to figure out more about it than anyone. She's got some kind of sixth sense."

"Don't be silly, Molly," Sarah said. "I'm just like everyone else."

Molly looked at Sarah and rolled her eyes. Then she began talking to her aunt eagerly. "I'm going to bring Sarah up to the Four Towers this afternoon. But let's not tell her anything yet. If there's something strange up there Sarah will know."

Caroline nodded her head seriously. "Some people can pick up on those things. From what Molly says, you seem like you'd be one of them."

Sarah started to protest, but Molly cut her off. "We already know what you're going to say, Sarah. But let's just wait and see. We'll visit the Four Towers this afternoon, and then, tonight, Aunt Caroline can tell us the entire legend. I want to see what you think without knowing the story. Anyway, it will be much better to have my aunt tell us about the Four Towers at night. It'll make it even creepier!"

Caroline smiled. "You always love a good story," she said to Molly. "But, if you want me to talk about the Four Towers, we'll have to find something to keep your uncle busy. You know he doesn't like it when I tell the old stories"

"I know," said Molly. "I'm sure we can find some work in the barn for him to do. We'll figure something out."

"Now," said Molly, grabbing Sarah's arm, "let's pack a lunch and get going. This is going to be a wonderful afternoon!"

"What do you want me to do if Arthur and Daniel arrive while you're gone?" asked Caroline. "You said you weren't sure if they were going to come out here this afternoon or in the evening."

"Send them after us," said Molly. "The more the merrier!"

\*\*\*\*\*

About half an hour later, Molly and Sarah were on their way. The afternoon was lovely. The weather was warm and pleasant and the sun was shining, a perfect summer day.

The two girls were on a well-worn trail that led from the farmhouse to the fields beyond and then up a gently sloping hill that bordered the back of the farm. The trail curved and wound its way up the hill, giving a beautiful view of the valley below.

"It's only about a twenty minute walk from the house," said Molly, as she walked beside Sarah. "It's always been one of my favorite places to go."

"I know you're sworn to secrecy," said Sarah, "but perhaps you could at least tell me where we're going."

Molly laughed, "I'll tell you a little, but you're not going to get the whole story out of me. You'll have to be patient until this evening. But for now, all you need to know is that the Four Towers are the ruins of an old castle."

"Oh," replied Sarah. "That sounds interesting enough for now."

"Perfect for a picnic," replied Molly. "And perhaps for more than that too, if you believe any of the stories that they tell around here."

"Stories that you aren't going to tell me," laughed Sarah.

"All in good time," replied Molly. "You'll love it without knowing anything about it. It's a very beautiful place."

"If it's as lovely as this," gestured Sarah, "I don't think I'll be disappointed.

The two girls had just crested a ridge, and, when they turned they could see the entire valley spread out below them.

"Are those your uncle's sheep?" asked Sarah.

A short distance away, they could see a flock of sheep being led up the hill by a dark figure.

"Yes," said Molly, looking in the direction that Sarah had indicated. "And that must be Jordan with them."

Molly and Sarah both waved at the youth. For a moment, it seemed as if he hadn't noticed them, but then, suddenly, he stopped and turned to look directly at the two girls. He stood there for several moments, staring intensely.

"I don't think he sees us," said Molly, waving again. "Or maybe he doesn't recognize us?"

Sarah looked towards the figure of Jordan and shivered. For a moment, she felt disconcerted. There was something about the way he was looking at them that made her nervous.

"He is a little odd, isn't he?" said Molly, noticing Sarah's reaction.

Finally, Jordan awoke from his trance and waved, as if

nothing out of the ordinary had happened.

"Maybe he's just not used to people," said Sarah, trying to put the best light on the situation.

"I guess hanging around sheep all the time would make anyone weird," laughed Molly. "You've met my uncle. He certainly isn't normal!"

*****

"I know you're going to love the Four Towers," said Molly, excitedly, as they turned another bend in the path.

"I hope we're almost there," said Sarah, looking up at the towering hills above. "Between the anticipation and all of these hills I don't know how much more I can take!"

Molly laughed. "Don't worry," she said, grabbing Sarah's arm. "We're really close."

Molly paused for a moment in speaking as she guided Sarah around a sharp curve in the road. There was a steep drop off on the left hand side of the path that Sarah hadn't even noticed until they were almost upon it.

"That's looks a little dangerous," said Sarah, nervously, edging closer to Molly.

"It is," said Molly. "That's why I was holding onto you. I don't know why they don't build a fence there, or something to warn people."

"It might ruin the charm of the place," said Sarah, with a laugh.

"Right," said Molly, "beautiful scenery comes before safety."

"You're going to have to duck down a little to get through," said Molly, with a gesture towards a rough stone formation that arched over the path.

Molly disappeared through the opening and Sarah bent down to follow her. As she did so, she heard Molly scream.

"Molly!" shouted Sarah. "What is it?"

Molly made no reply. Sarah swallowed her fear and plunged after her friend, not knowing what she would find on other side.

# CHAPTER III
# THE FOUR TOWERS

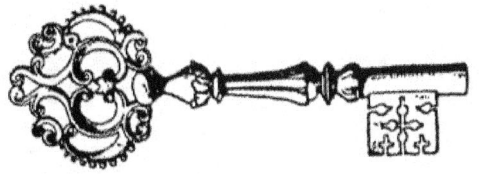

olly!" said Sarah, struggling to get through the narrow opening as fast as she could. "What happened? Are you okay?"

It took a moment for Sarah's eyes to adjust as she emerged into the sunlight on the other side of the pass. As they did so, she made out the figures of Molly, and two other people. Who were they? And what were they doing here?

Suddenly, Sarah realized who the two strangers were.

"Arthur! Daniel!" said Sarah, surprised. "What are you doing?"

Scaring me half to death," said Molly.

"It wasn't our idea," said Arthur. "I swear!"

"It's true," agreed Daniel. "We're innocent. It was your Uncle Jacob's idea. We showed up at the house to surprise you this morning, but you had just left. Jacob gave us a ride to the other side of the ruins, and then we walked the rest of the way here. He told us about the pass. He thought we could catch you right as you came out of the passage and surprise you."

"Well, he was right, but not in a good way," said Molly. "I'm not going to let either of you get away with this."

"What are you going to do?" laughed Daniel.

"I have lunch," said Molly, brandishing the basket that her aunt had packed that morning. "And there's only enough for two! That means me and Sarah, not the two of you!"

"Sorry to disappoint you," laughed Arthur, "but your aunt is one step ahead of you." Arthur lifted his arm to show the girls an identical basket to the one Molly held.

"I can't win," said Molly. "But just wait...we'll get back at you two at some point, won't we Sarah?"

Sarah, who was standing nearby, seemed hardly to have heard the conversation. She was staring at the ruins of the castle in the valley below.

"Sorry, Molly," said Sarah. "I got distracted." She gestured towards the castle ruins. "It's beautiful, but in a very sad way."

"Oh, I know!" said Molly. "If these two hadn't ruined our entrance, it would have been even more spectacular. It's incredible to come out of the passage and see the ruins spread out in front of you."

"There's such a lonely feel about the place," said Sarah, looking around. "But it's still so lovely."

"I'm glad you can appreciate it," said Molly. "Some people think it's just a pile of old rocks."

"I may be one of them," laughed Daniel. "I hardly noticed it, and we've been here half an hour waiting for you."

"Can we get a little closer?" asked Arthur, curiously. "I'd like to see it up close."

"Of course," said Molly. "We have all morning to explore. And then, when we get hungry, we can find a nice place to have our picnic."

The four began walking towards the castle ruins, talking as they went.

"I wanted to be there when you met my aunt and uncle," Molly said. "I hope they didn't say anything to embarrass me. I can't even imagine what Uncle Jacob asked you, Daniel!"

"I think he almost has us married by now," said Daniel, laughingly. "But your aunt was very nice."

"You're not allowed to be alone with them again! At least not with Uncle Jacob," said Molly. "He's a bad influence on you. He already had you scare us! Who knows what other ideas he's going to come up with?"

Sarah laughed and said, "Regardless of your scaring us half to death, we're both glad you're here now. We didn't know when you were going to arrive or we would have waited for you."

"Speaking of the village," said Molly, "I hope your first night was peaceful."

"It was," said Arthur. "Very quiet and peaceful," smiled Arthur. "Just the way I like it."

"How do you like Mrs. Bannerbee?" asked Molly. "She's a good friend of my aunt and uncle."

"She couldn't be nicer," said Daniel. "It's like staying with my grandmother. I think we're both going to be spoiled by the time we leave."

"You already are spoiled," laughed Molly. "I hope Mrs. Bannerbee doesn't make things any worse!"

Sarah laughed and then paused for a moment to admire the ruins ahead. Suddenly, she stopped dead in her tracks. There was something wrong.

"What's the matter?" asked Arthur.

"Molly," asked Sarah curiously, "isn't this supposed to be called the Four Towers?"

"Yes," answered Molly, with a mysterious smile.

"Perhaps I'm wrong," said Sarah, "but I only see three."

Arthur and Daniel looked towards the ruins as well.

"You're right," said Arthur. "There are only three towers."

"How did we miss that?" said Daniel. "We walked right by it."

"Well," said Molly "you're the one who thought it was just a pile of old rocks! But you're going to have to wait until tonight. My Aunt Caroline is going to tell us the entire legend of the Four Towers this evening. For now, let's just say that appearances can be deceiving."

"This better be one good story," said Sarah.

"Don't worry...it is," replied Molly.

The four had just reached the walls of the ruined castle.

"You need to walk around the castle walls first before going inside to really appreciate it," said Molly, as she grabbed Daniel's arm and led him towards the far wall.

Sarah and Arthur let Molly and Daniel go ahead without

them. They both wanted to take a moment to admire the ruins. Before them, was a massive rectangle of gray stone, crumbling in places, but still stern and forbidding. At three of the corners of the castle walls were towers, in various stages of decay. However, at the far corner of the ruins, where there should have been a fourth tower, there was nothing, just a large gap in the stone wall.

Sarah and Arthur gazed at the castle in silent wonder. There was something almost magical about the ruins, despite the damage of time.

Just then, Sarah and Arthur were interrupted by a shout from above. They looked up to see Molly and Daniel standing on the parapet above them.

"You should join us!" said Daniel. "The view is incredible from up here."

"Sounds like a good idea," said Arthur eagerly.

"The stairs are to your left, at the base of the first tower," said Molly. "And don't worry...they're safe. It's the only tower you can still climb."

Sarah looked up at the crumbling castle walls and shivered.

"I think I'll wait here," she said. "You know I don't like heights."

"You sure you're okay down here by yourself?" asked Arthur. "I don't mind staying with you if you want."

"I'm fine," said Sarah. "I'll look around inside while you're up there."

"Okay," said Arthur, as he walked towards the tower stairs. "But yell if you need anything."

Sarah walked slowly through the large arched gate, which served as the entrance to the castle grounds. As she entered the castle, the sunlight grew dimmer, blocked by the thick walls and towers. It was very quiet and solemn.

"It's amazing," said Sarah to herself, softly. "It's so much bigger than it seemed from the outside. You could get lost in here."

Sarah made her way across the enclosed space of the

courtyard. It was clear that at one time there were rooms and walls in the area through which she was walking.

"I can't imagine what it was like when people lived here," said Sarah. "It must have been beautiful!"

As Sarah spoke, she reached the space where the fourth tower should have been. There was a faint circular outline on the rutted stone floor. However, there were no ruins or tumbled down rocks indicating that anything had ever stood in the spot.

"Beautiful...and just a little creepy," added Sarah, as she gazed at the strange, empty space.

Suddenly, Sarah noticed something odd happening. The circle on the floor that marked the tower's boundary appeared to be getting darker and more defined.

Sarah looked away and rubbed her eyes. It had to be a trick of the light or some other illusion.

"I must be imagining things!" she said to herself. "All of these strange stories are getting to me...."

Sarah trailed off and gasped. The floor was getting darker! There was no doubt about it now. Suddenly, a bright, angry glow appeared in the space before her, outlining the tower's foundation.

Sarah could feel her heart beating faster. She looked down at her ring, but it wasn't giving her any sign or warning. It looked normal. She took a deep breath and gathered her courage. She wanted to see if she could sense what it was that was causing such a strange disturbance.

Sarah directed all of her attention on the glowing circle on the floor before her. She didn't sense any immediate danger. But there was definitely something there. Something evil that had been disturbed. After a few moments, the strange circle on the floor faded and soon there was nothing left, except the faint outline that Sarah had seen when she first approached the fourth tower.

At that moment a man leaped from behind the wall, shouting the gesturing.

"You shouldn't be here!" he yelled. "It's not safe!"

Sarah stood shocked and aghast before the strange man. He was cavorting about the castle wall like a madman.

"I don't want to hear any excuses or explanations! This is a dangerous haunted place! I tell everyone I see here to stay away and never come again. Bad things happen here! This castle is cursed!"

The man paused for a moment and glared directly at Sarah.

"And you!" he shouted. "You're bad for this place. You're disturbing things that should be left to rest. Begone!"

Sarah, still at a loss for words, ran across the castle courtyard and out through the gate. She took a few deep breaths as she emerged into the open air. What had happened back there? And who was that strange man? Before Sarah had time to collect her thoughts, Molly, Daniel, and Arthur joined her at the castle gate.

"You missed out," said Arthur. "The views from the top of the castle walls are incredible."

Sarah smiled weakly. "I thought I was choosing the safer course by staying down here, but I think I was wrong. I was chased out by a very strange man."

"Oh no," groaned Molly. "You met crazy Jonas Pickering. I should have warned you. He's harmless, but he's very annoying. He hangs out up here at the ruins, harassing everyone he meets..."

Before Molly could say anything else, Jonas Pickering suddenly appeared before them, leaping out from behind an angle in the castle wall.

"Aha!" he shouted. "There are more of you!"

"Jonas," protested Molly, "what are you trying to do? You already scared one of my friends half to death! And now you're sneaking up on us! You can't do these things."

Jonas took off his well-worn hat and made an elaborate bow. "I'm sorry my dear, but it had to be done. You know you shouldn't go meddling about this place. There are dark forces here..."

"We were just about to have lunch," interrupted Molly, hoping to cut off the loquacious Jonas. But old Jonas was not to be put off.

"I'm surprised you have any appetite," he said. "How could you think about eating when you're so close to this cursed place? It's dangerous here, there are dark forces at work..."

Suddenly Jonas stopped in mid-sentence and jerked himself around, facing the ruins of the castle. "And the dark forces are here now! Only I can stop them! Beware and keep away!"

With that parting warning, Jonas ran back through the gate and into the castle grounds.

"Ugh," sighed Molly. "Sorry about that....just one of the crazy locals."

"Do you think he'll come back?" asked Sarah, worriedly.

"I doubt it," said Molly, who was leading her friends away from the castle to one of her favorite scenic spots for a picnic lunch.

"Usually one warning a day is enough for Jonas. He sleeps up here too, which is probably what he's about to do now. I'm pretty sure we'll be gone by the time he wakes up."

*****

A few moments later, the four friends were sitting peacefully on a ridge overlooking the castle. Molly was busy unpacking the two baskets that her aunt had provided for lunch.

"This is a feast!" said Molly, as she spread out the provisions on the blanket. "My aunt must think there are more than four of us!"

"Nonsense!" said Arthur, grabbing a large handful of grapes and popping them into his mouth. "I could eat most of this food by myself."

"Well, you're going to have to share," laughed Molly.

"That's okay," said Arthur, as he started to devour his sandwich. "I'll eat fast. That way I'll get more!"

"Let's enjoy our lunch and then we can head back to my aunt and uncle's house," said Molly, ignoring Arthur. "We can take the long way home and walk through the village if you'd like."

"That would be wonderful," replied Sarah. "I'd love to see the village in the daylight. I was half asleep when the train arrived last night. I know it's supposed to be very pretty."

"Oh yes," said Molly, settling herself more comfortably on the blanket. "Castleton is a beautiful little village. I know you'll love it."

*****

On the walk back, Sarah lagged behind, letting Molly and Daniel take the lead. She wanted to talk to Arthur without any chance of being overheard.

"What's wrong?" said Arthur. "You've been really quiet since lunch. Did that crazy old Pickering fellow really scare you?

"It's more than Jonas Pickering," said Sarah, reluctantly. "There was something else, something that I saw in the castle."

Arthur smiled and looked at Sarah. "Is the place really haunted like they say?"

"No, nothing like that," said Sarah, with a slight smile, "I didn't see any ghosts if that's what you're thinking."

"Then what was it?" asked Arthur, with concern. "Something scared you."

"I don't know how to explain it exactly," said Sarah. "But when I was by myself in the castle, I saw something strange where the fourth tower was supposed to be. The ground started glowing and I could sense something evil."

"Ugh," groaned Arthur. "That doesn't sound good. I thought we were supposed to be on vacation. Didn't we have enough excitement last fall at Westmere?"

"I don't think Guardians are ever on vacation," said Sarah, half smiling. "Isn't that what Uncle Alfred always says?"

"Anyway, there may be nothing to worry about," she continued. "As we both know, there are lots of places in the world like this. Places that are better left undisturbed. But I don't think it would hurt to contact my uncle, just to be sure. He might know something about this place. Or at least he could find out for us."

Arthur sighed. "Alright," he said. "I guess it's better to be safe than sorry. But I just spent the last month with your uncle. It was great, but I need a break!"

"I understand," said Sarah, "I'll talk to him. On the way through the village we can stop and I'll call him. I'm probably just being silly anyway. I'm sure there's nothing for us to worry about."

# CHAPTER IV
# THE LEGEND

 hat evening, the four friends were gathered in the parlor of the old farmhouse. They had just finished dinner and were happily recounting the adventures of the day to Jacob and Caroline.

"Crazy old Jonas Pickering nearly scared Sarah out of her senses. He chased her out of the castle yelling all sorts of crazy things," said Molly.

Jacob's brow creased in annoyance. "That man is a nuisance, scaring people and ranting and raving like a lunatic! He's been spreading his Four Towers nonsense around the entire county for years. Something needs to be done about him."

"It's alright," said Sarah. "I survived, so I guess he's not that bad."

Jacob scowled, and then got up from his place on the sofa reluctantly.

"I hate to leave such good company, but I have an early day tomorrow and I need to get to bed. You young people keep much later hours than we do in the country."

"Are you coming, Caroline?" he asked his wife.

"I think I'll stay up a little longer," she said. "It's not often that I get to see Molly and her friends."

"Alright," said Jacob, giving his wife a hug. "I'll see you in the morning then."

As soon as Jacob was gone, Molly and Caroline exchanged a conspiratorial glance.

"Now you'll finally get to hear about the legend of the Four Towers!" said Molly, excitedly. "No one can tell the story like my aunt."

Caroline smiled at Molly's excitement. "I don't know if the story is as incredible as Molly is making it out to be, but I think you'll enjoy hearing it. Jacob says it's all a bunch of nonsense, but I've lived here my whole life and I know that there's truth to the old legends."

At that moment, Jordan entered the room. "Sorry to interrupt," he said, looking around the room uncomfortably. "I was looking for Jacob."

"He's gone to bed for the night," replied Caroline. "Was it anything important?"

"It can wait until the morning," muttered Jordan, already half out of the room.

"Wait," said Caroline, "you're welcome to join us."

"I still have work to do..." he began.

"But Aunt Caroline was just about to tell us the story of the Four Towers," interrupted Molly. "You have to stay!"

At the mention of the Four Towers, Jordan's face changed. He looked torn between wanting to leave and wanting to stay. Finally, he said, "Maybe I could stay, but only for a little while."

"You won't regret it," said Molly. "Aunt Caroline is the best storyteller I know!"

As Molly spoke, Caroline dimmed the lights in the already darkened room and lit several candles on the table. "The story is always better by candlelight," she said, softly before settling down into her chair and beginning her tale.

"A long, long time ago, a noble family by the name of Montclair began to build a castle, the ruins of which you saw today. They were long inhabitants of this area of England and held dominance over all. At the time of my story, Edward Montclair was the head of the family. He was a young man and had just come into possession of the entire estate. Before his inheritance, he had spent several years traveling throughout Europe. When he returned to England, he brought a young bride back with him named Caroline."

"Caroline and Edward seemed destined for happiness. He was devoted to her and she loved him deeply. Edward brought his bride to the family castle. The Montclairs had been living in the castle for hundreds of years, but it was still rough and unfinished. Edward wanted to make the castle a splendid palace for his beloved bride. He outdid himself providing every comfort for Caroline. But his crowning achievement was to be the completion of the fourth tower. The castle had originally been designed to have four towers, one at each corner of the outer wall. None of Edward's predecessors had ever finished building the fourth tower. But Edward was determined to finish the castle for his love."

"About a year into their marriage, Edward, who had been hard at work on his renovations, suddenly stopped. The tower still wasn't finished, but Edward didn't seem to care. He started spending all of his time alone and he became distant and unpleasant to everyone around him. Caroline was devastated. She yearned for the companionship of her beloved husband. But Edward had become obsessed with darker pursuits."

"The change in Edward had occurred right around the time that he acquired a strange artifact from a traveling peddler. At first, Edward saw the item as an interesting curiosity, nothing more. However, as he delved deeper into the item's mysterious past, it took hold of him. Edward began spending all of his time in a small study at the end of the courtyard, away from the main area of the castle. He started conducting bizarre experiments. Dark smoke and strange odors poured out of his study constantly. He barely ate or slept, he was so wrapped up in the object that he had found."

"What was it?" interrupted Jordan, anxiously.

Everyone turned and looked at him, surprised that he had spoken. Caroline however, looked gratified at his question. She enjoyed having a captive audience.

"That is the questions, isn't it?" she said, mysteriously. "No one really knows for sure. There are many theories, but, personally I think the item that Edward found was the philosopher's stone."

"What's the philosopher's stone?" asked Arthur, curiously.

"The creation of a philosopher's stone was the goal of the alchemists," said Caroline. "It was supposed to be able to turn metals into gold or silver. But beyond that, it had other even more incredible properties, such as lengthening life and perhaps even conferring immortality."

"But that's impossible," said Daniel. "The philosopher's stone isn't real."

"That's what some people think," said Caroline, "but I don't agree with them. We've lost the wisdom of the past in modern times. Things that were very real long ago seem impossible now, especially to scientists."

"I guess," said Daniel, doubtfully. "But alchemy has been disproven. There isn't some magical substance that can turn metals into gold."

Molly laughed. "Daniel is our scientist," she said. "He's very rational, especially when it comes to chemistry. It's his favorite subject."

"It's not that I don't believe in things that seem impossible," protested Daniel. "I've seen some things myself that can't be explained," he added, with a significant glance at Arthur and Sarah.

"But," he continued, "alchemy and the philosopher's stone just don't work with modern science."

"Regardless," said Caroline, with a smile, "there's no way to know for sure what Edward was up to. As I said before, it's just my opinion that he found the philosopher's stone. There's no proof."

"But what happened to the stone?" asked Jordan eagerly,

again breaking his normal reserve.

Caroline smiled at him. "It's the best part of the story," she said.

"Caroline had been worrying about her husband for some time. She had watched the man she married gradually turn into an evil, spiteful monster. She had tried everything she could to make Edward give up his obsession, but to no avail. To make matters worse, disturbing things were happening at the castle. Caroline was restless and many nights, when she couldn't sleep, she spent the night wandering about. On one of these nights, she saw it...the ghostly outline of the fourth tower! Edward hadn't finished building the fourth tower, yet there it was, strange and shadowy, looming out at her in the darkness.

"One day, when Edward had been called away into town on business, Caroline snuck into his study. I don't know how much she understood of what Edward was doing, but from what she saw, she knew the stone had to be destroyed before something horrible happened. That evening, before Edward returned, she took the stone. She didn't know what she was going to do, but she knew she had to get the stone away from her husband. As she was leaving the study with the stone, Edward returned. He saw her and began chasing her along the castle parapet. Caroline ran as fast as she could, but the stone greatly impeded her progress. She felt as if it was trying to slow her down.

"Finally, Caroline made it to the end of the wall, where the fourth tower was making its regular nightly appearance. She prayed for some type of intervention to save her from the wrath of her husband and the evil of the stone. Suddenly, the area at the bottom of the fourth tower opened up before her. Angry flames leapt from the opening, almost reaching to the top of the tower. That was it! She could throw the stone into the flames below. But, try as she might, the stone wouldn't budge. In despair, Caroline realized that she was going to have to destroy herself along with the stone. With Edward only a few feet behind her, Caroline jumped into the flames holding tightly to the stone. Overcome with madness at the loss of the stone, Edward jumped after her."

"Yikes!" Molly shivered. "No matter how many times I hear this story it still scares me."

Sarah looked thoughtful. "What happened to the castle after that?"

"It was abandoned by the Montclair family. That's why it's in such a ruined state today," said Caroline. "No one wanted to live there after such a tragedy. And of course, there was the fourth tower to deter people."

"What about the fourth tower?" asked Sarah curiously.

"Ever since Caroline and Edward's deaths, there have been strange sightings and disturbances at the castle. Many people have claimed that they've seen the fourth tower. There are weird lights and flashes that appear over the place. And animals are terrified of the area. I don't know if you noticed while you were there, but you'll never see any animals, not even birds, on the castle grounds."

"But what happened to the stone?" asked Jordan, impatiently. "Did anyone ever find it?"

"It was never found," said Caroline. "Some think it was destroyed when Caroline jumped into the flames. Others think it might still be somewhere on the grounds of the castle. To this day no one knows for certain."

"It probably never existed in the first place," said Daniel.

"Don't go and ruin the story!" said Molly.

"I'm just pointing out the facts," laughed Daniel.

"Well," said Caroline, "I think Jordan....," she paused and looked over to where Jordan had been sitting just a moment before. "Oh, he's gone," she said in surprise. "I didn't even see him leave."

"I don't think any of us did," said Arthur, looking around the darkened room.

"He seemed more interested in staring at Sarah and asking weird questions about the stone than actually listening to the story," giggled Molly.

"I didn't notice him staring at me," said Sarah, feeling slightly uncomfortable.

"Well he was," said Molly. "You may not have noticed, but I did. He's definitely a strange one!"

"Oh Molly," said Caroline. "You think everyone's strange. He's just a little shy. That makes him seem awkward."

Molly rolled her eyes at her aunt.

"And now," said Caroline, "since the story is done, I think it's about time for dessert! Would you two mind helping me?" she asked, looking at Molly and Daniel.

"Of course not," said Molly, jumping up to follow her aunt into the kitchen.

"Anything that involves dessert is good with me," said Daniel, enthusiastically. "I'm an experienced taste tester."

"I don't think that will be necessary," laughed Molly.

"We'll be right back," she said to Sarah and Arthur. "Don't get too scared in here while we're gone!"

"Well," said Arthur, softly, as soon as they had left the room, "at least we know a little bit more about the Four Towers. I wonder if anything that Molly's aunt said was connected to what you saw this afternoon."

"I don't know," said Sarah slowly. "Uncle Alfred didn't seem to think there was much to worry about, but I'm not so sure."

"What exactly did Alfred tell you?" asked Arthur, curiously. "We didn't have a chance to talk after you called him."

"Oh," said Sarah, "I forgot you didn't know. He already knew about the Four Towers. In fact, the Guardians have sent people here before, but nothing real has ever happened. The disturbances in the past were just locals playing tricks in order to attract more visitors to the site. But I don't know. It didn't feel like that to me."

"What does he want us to do?" asked Arthur.

"He said to be careful. He doesn't want us to have another Westmere on our hands! But for now, he didn't think we should be too alarmed. He wants us to gather as much information as we can about the Four Towers. But he doesn't want us spending time at the Towers themselves. He also gave me the name of someone we can talk to in the village, an old man who he's known for a long time. He's not a Guardian, but he's friendly to our group."

"Your uncle knows people everywhere," said Arthur, in amazement.

Sarah laughed. "I know," she said. "I guess that's a benefit of being a Guardian for so long."

"And what do you think of what Caroline said about the philosopher's stone?" asked Arthur.

"I don't know," said Sarah, sounding doubtful. "I'm inclined to agree with Daniel. I didn't think it was something that really existed."

"Do you know anything about it?" asked Arthur.

"Not much," replied Sarah. "You would think we'd both know more. It's a trendy subject in all of those best-selling teen fantasy books."

"That's what we get for not reading popular books!" laughed Arthur.

"Well anyway, I think it's about time we became experts on the philosopher's stone and the Four Towers," said Sarah.

"We can do research in the village," said Arthur. "They actually have some modern technology there," he smiled.

"Unlike out here in the country," laughed Sarah. "And maybe we can visit Uncle Alfred's friend tomorrow. He may be able to point us in the right direction."

"Sounds like a plan," said Arthur, "Although I'm still upset we're not really on vacation."

"Like I keep saying," smiled Sarah, "guardians are never on vacation. Trouble tends to find us wherever we go!"

# CHAPTER V
# PRITCHARDS

he next morning, Sarah woke with a start. She had intended to get up early. But, when she looked at her clock, it was already well past ten. How had she slept so late? A late evening plus all of the previous day's excitement at the Four Towers must have tired her out.

"Ugh," Sarah groaned, "I'm not going to get anything done today."

As Sarah got out of bed, she heard a loud strident voice from the rooms below. It sounded exactly like Margaret Pritchard. Was it possible? Molly had mentioned that Margaret might visit, but Sarah hadn't believed her. The Margaret that Sarah knew would never willingly take a trip to a farm in a tiny village in England. She was much too cosmopolitan for that.

Suddenly, an unmistakable, high-pitched voice overpowered Margaret's harsher tones. It sounded exactly like Eustace, Margaret's younger brother. Were they really both downstairs? Sarah knew that Eustace was spending the summer in Paris, studying to be a pastry chef. A visit from Eustace made much more sense to Sarah. He was helplessly in love with Molly and had been for years. Perhaps he had dragged Margaret along with him on his trip.

As soon as Sarah was ready, she rushed down the stairs

and into the kitchen. "My ears didn't deceive me," she smiled. "I thought I heard the two of you!"

There, seated at the large wooden table, was Margaret, in all her glory. Eustace was also in the kitchen, hovering over the oven with Caroline.

"Surprise!" said Margaret, standing up as Sarah entered the room. "I didn't want to come, but Eustace made me. I would give you a hug, but you know I don't like hugging people."

"It's nice to see you too," said Sarah, walking over to Margaret and hugging her anyway.

"It's not that I didn't want to see any of you," Margaret began, "it's just that I don't really like the country. And I have so many more important things I need to be doing right now. But Eustace insisted. You know how annoying he can be," she said.

"Hey," said Eustace, looking over at this sister, "I can hear you, you know."

Margaret rolled her eyes at Sarah and sighed in frustration. "He's impossible," she said.

Sarah smiled. Margaret and Eustace were always at odds. Margaret was constantly bemoaning the fact that her brother was a pathetic excuse for a Pritchard. The Pritchards were an old, established family, characterized by their aggressiveness and ruthless attitudes towards others. Eustace had none of these traits.

But, looking at him today, Sarah thought that Margaret was missing something. In the past few months, Eustace had shot up in height, and was no longer the puny pipsqueak that Margaret still called him. In addition, his hair, once shockingly red, had darkened quite a bit to a lovely auburn shade. To Sarah's surprise, he was becoming handsome! His personality hadn't changed. He was still awkwardly outspoken and overly enthusiastic about everything. And he still had the same high-pitched squeaky voice and flamboyant taste in clothing. Perhaps those things didn't make him a good Pritchard, but they did make him very endearing.

"Eustace is showing me how to make pastry," said Caroline, with a loving glance at the boy she had just met. "He's incredible!"

Margaret rolled her eyes again. "For some reason middle-aged women love him," she whispered. "It's really weird."

"How long are you staying?" asked Sarah, trying to change the subject away from Eustace.

"A few days," said Margaret, "maybe a week at the most. Eustace has to get back to his ridiculous pastry chef classes next week. Who ever heard of a Pritchard becoming a pastry chef? It's demeaning! He's dragging the family name down!"

Margaret shot an angry glance at Eustace and then continued, "And I need to be back too. I'm in the middle of a project and it's really important that I get it done. In fact, I'm going to have to work on it while I'm here."

Sarah smiled. "That doesn't surprise me. I wouldn't expect anything less of a Pritchard."

"By the way," she continued, glancing around the kitchen. "Where's Molly? Does she know you're here?"

"Molly!" squeaked Eustace. "I still haven't seen her!"

"She went out early this morning with her uncle and Jordan to do some work around the farm," replied Caroline, looking compassionately at the lovelorn Eustace.

"You could have gone after them," snapped Margaret, "so I don't think you have anything to complain about."

"What?!" said Eustace, his face suddenly terror stricken. "That would have been too dangerous. Farm animals hate me. How would you feel if I was attacked by a crazy sheep?"

Margaret shrugged her shoulders. "I don't think I would mind too much," she replied.

"Well," added Caroline, with a significant look at Margaret, "Eustace didn't go, but Margaret's friend went after them."

"Friend?" said Sarah in surprise. Margaret was not known for her friendships. "Did you bring someone with you?"

Margaret scowled and looked uncomfortable. "I had to," she said. "He's my partner for this project that I'm working on.

If he didn't come with me, I wouldn't be able to get anything done."

"He?!" said Sarah, her interest piqued.

"Yes, he," answered Caroline, with a smile. "He's extremely good looking and he seems very interested in Margaret, and not because of a shared business project. He has a lovely accent too. Where did you say he was from?"

Margaret squirmed in her seat. "South Africa," she answered. "And I hadn't noticed his accent or his looks. He's just another intern at the company."

"I think you might be blushing," said Sarah, laughing.

"Margaret has a boyfriend! Margaret has a boyfriend!" shouted Eustace, as he danced around the kitchen, brandishing a rolling pin.

"Eustace" said Margaret threateningly, "if you don't shut up right now I promise that I'll...."

Before Margaret could finish speaking, Jacob, Molly, and someone whom Sarah had never seen before entered the kitchen.

The newcomer had to be Margaret's "boyfriend." He was very tall and well built. He had dark skin and his eyes were dark and piercing. Caroline was right about his looks. He was incredibly handsome.

"Good morning everyone," said Jacob, cheerfully. "I see you're all finally awake."

"I intended to get up much earlier," smiled Sarah. "I don't know what happened."

"You missed a good morning's work on the farm," answered Jacob. "This wonderful young man is an extremely hard worker."

Margaret's "boyfriend" smiled at Jacob's compliment, a radiant smile that lit up his entire face. "My grandparents have a farm in South Africa. I used to spend a lot of time there."

"You must be Sarah," he continued. "Margaret's told me so much about you. I'm Thato, but you can call me Tad....everyone else does."

Sarah smiled and extended her hand in greeting. "It's so nice to meet you. I can't imagine what Margaret said about me, but I'm just going to assume it was all good."

"Most of it was good," said Margaret. "Of course, I didn't tell him everything that happened at Westmere."

"That's probably smart," answered Sarah. "You actually did a few nice things for me there. I wouldn't want Tad to get the wrong idea."

"Exactly what I was thinking," Margaret replied.

During all of this time, Eustace was standing speechless, still hanging on to the rolling pin. He was staring at Molly adoringly, who he hadn't seen in several months.

Finally, Molly noticed him. "Hi Eustace," she said, in amusement.

"Hey," he said awkwardly, his face radiant. "You look lovely."

Molly laughed and looked down at her clothes, begrimed from the farm work she had been doing with her uncle. "You really think so?"

"Of course," answered Eustace. "You always look lovely."

"Ugh!" groaned Margaret. "Can we stop all this nonsense? Eustace, weren't you supposed to be making us something to eat for breakfast?" she said.

"Right," said Eustace, his mind diverted from Molly back to the joys of pastry. "You're going to love these! They're chocolate croissants...my own secret recipe. If everyone would sit down, I'll serve you the best pastries you've ever had!"

"He's not kidding," said Caroline, "I tried one. They're heavenly!"

"Any pastry is a good pastry, in my opinion," said Jacob, as he sat down at the table, "as long as you made a lot. I'm starving!"

As everyone scrambled to get a seat at the table, Sarah noticed that Tad made a point of sitting next to Margaret, who appeared to be ignoring him. Eustace, with a platter of pastries in hand, was also quick to locate a seat next to Molly. Sarah smiled to herself. Love was certainly in the air.

"Where are Arthur and Daniel?" asked Margaret. "Aren't they supposed to be here too?"

"They're staying in town," said Molly. "I thought we could head over there after breakfast and spend the afternoon with them. I don't want you to get bored in the country."

Margaret looked relieved. "That's a good idea," she said. "All of this fresh air is making me nervous."

Sarah smiled. Molly's plan was perfect! Despite oversleeping, she would still be able to get into the village. Hopefully she and Arthur would have time to talk to Alfred's friend. Perhaps he would be able to throw some light on the mysterious Four Towers.

*****

About an hour later, Margaret and Sarah were standing outside, waiting for Molly, Eustace, and Tad to join them. Eustace was helping Caroline finish the clean-up in the kitchen while Molly was giving Tad a quick tour of the house before they left for town.

Margaret looked out at the fields, where sheep and cows were grazing, and shuddered. "Yuck!" she said. "I don't know how anyone could live on a farm. It's so....rural!"

"Jacob and Caroline seem to like it," said Sarah. "And it is very peaceful here."

"A little too peaceful," said Margaret. "All of this peace and quiet makes me feel anxious."

Just then, Jordan passed in front of the two girls on his way to the barn. He paused when he saw them, stared fixedly at Sarah for a moment, and then looked away and hurried on.

"Jordan, wait!" said Sarah, trying to get him to stop.

Jordan paused again, fixed Sarah with the same intense stare, and then continued on his way.

"I was going to introduce you," said Sarah. "He's one of Jacob's helpers on the farm."

44

"I think Caroline mentioned him this morning," said Margaret, thoughtfully, looking after the retreating figure. "He's a bit odd. The way he was staring at you...."

"He's shy," answered Sarah, "and Molly seems to think he has a crush on me."

"No," said Margaret. "He wasn't looking at you like that."

"Well, you definitely aren't one to flatter a girl's vanity," smiled Sarah.

"Don't be silly," snapped Margaret. "I'm not saying that no one likes you. I just don't think he's looking at you in that way. He's interested in you, that's obvious, but for some other reason."

"You're starting to make me a little nervous," laughed Sarah.

"I'm not trying to," said Margaret. "But I've been working on business relationships all summer for my internship. I've gotten good at reading people's faces. And his is very interesting. I can't quite make it out."

As Margaret was speaking, Molly and Tad emerged from the house.

"I just want to show Tad the barn," said Molly, "and then we can go."

"The barn!" said Margaret, in disgust, as soon as the two were out of earshot. "Why would you want to see a barn? There's something seriously wrong with Tad."

"I don't know about that," said Sarah, with a smile, "except for the fact that he's completely in love with you."

Margaret sighed in frustration. "I don't have time for boyfriends," she scowled.

Margaret looked at Sarah and her face suddenly became serious.

"You know Sarah," she said, "you and I....we're not like everyone else. Neither of us is going to settle down and be ordinary. You know what I'm like...I have bigger plans for my life. And you're not like anyone else I've ever met before. We're different."

Sarah nodded slowly. She knew exactly what Margaret was talking about. It was something she had been struggling with for some time. Being a Guardian and dealing with all of the responsibilities that it entailed was becoming more and more difficult for her.

"I know," answered Sarah seriously. She paused for a moment and sighed. "Sometimes I don't know if that's a good thing or a bad thing."

"I think it's a good thing," said Margaret, firmly. "I don't want to be like everyone else, boring and stupid! Anyway, if I did have time for boyfriends right now, I would definitely not want one like Tad!"

"But what's wrong with him?" protested Sarah. "He looks like a male model, he seems really nice, and he must be smart or he wouldn't be an intern with you."

"That's the problem," grumbled Margaret. "He's way too nice!"

Sarah laughed. "Oh I see. Only you would say that!"

"It's not just that I don't like nice people," said Margaret. "His niceness is ruining our project!"

"How is being nice a problem for your project?" asked Sarah.

"We're supposed to be working on how Pritchard Enterprises can expand over the next ten years. I've found several businesses that I know would be much more profitable if they were part of Pritchard Enterprises. I want to design our project around a hostile takeover of these businesses. But Tad doesn't think it's a good idea. He just doesn't get it!"

"Oh, I think I understand," said Sarah slowly. "So if Tad saw things your way, you might give him a chance."

"Maybe," said Margaret. "I still wouldn't want him as a boyfriend, but at least I could tolerate him. Right now, everything he does gets on my nerves. If he could just have a little more backbone...."

"Be more like a Pritchard, maybe," smiled Sarah.

"Exactly," replied Margaret. "He needs some of the

Pritchard cold-heartedness."

Just then, Eustace stumbled out of the house, almost falling on the ground next to them.

"Oops!" giggled Eustace. "I didn't see that step. It's a good thing I didn't fall. I might have really hurt myself...and messed up my clothes."

"I definitely don't want him to be a Pritchard like Eustace," moaned Margaret.

"What's wrong with me?" squeaked Eustace. "I'm just as good a Pritchard as you are. Plus I have way more friends than you and everyone likes me more."

"That's just my point Eustace," said Margaret. "A good Pritchard has enemies, not friends."

Before the discussion between Eustace and Margaret could escalate into an argument, Tad and Molly emerged from the barn.

"It's a really beautiful place they have here," said Tad. "You should have looked at the barn with me," he said to Margaret.

"Oh no!" said Eustace, with an alarmed glance in the direction of the barn. "That's not possible. Pritchards don't like barns."

"I think that's one thing we can both agree on," said Margaret.

"If you're all ready," said Molly, "I think we can get going. My uncle said he'd drive us into town."

"Yippee!" said Eustace. "No more walking!"

# CHAPTER VI
# THE TOWN

rthur sighed and looked at his watch again.
"Late, as usual," he muttered to himself.
Margaret had called him from the farm about
an hour ago. They had made arrangements for
everyone to meet up in the town square at noon. It was now
half past and there was still no sign of his friends.

Arthur was trying not to feel frustrated, but it was difficult.
He hated waiting. To make matters worse, he was alone.
Daniel had remained behind to help Mrs. Bannerbee repair a
broken window. In only a few days, Daniel had become fast
friends with Mrs. Bannerbee, the elderly woman in whose
house they were staying. It was just like Daniel to always go
out of his way to do nice things for people. He had assured
Arthur that he would join him as quickly as he could.
Hopefully it would be soon.

Arthur looked around the town square and scowled. It was
a beautiful summer day. There was supposed to be a storm
later, although it didn't seem possible at the moment. The sky
was a beautiful blue with only a few stray clouds and the air
was fresh and clean. Arthur's mood, however, was more in line
with an impending storm.

"Maybe there's more going on here than I think," said
Arthur to himself. He had felt uneasy since he woke up that
morning. Strange dreams which he only vaguely remember

had disturbed his sleep the previous night. He was troubled and irritable.

"It's just like I felt at Westmere," he muttered. Arthur had sensed the disturbances at Westmere Academy even before he knew anything about the Guardians and his own powers. The evil at Westmere had made him ill at ease and angry, just like he felt now.

"It has to be the Four Towers," he said. "There's something about the place which just doesn't feel right."

Arthur hoped that he would get a chance to talk to Sarah alone that afternoon. He wanted to find out if she was feeling the same way he was. And, the sooner they were able to speak with Alfred's friend, the better.

"And now we have London to worry about too," Arthur remembered suddenly, with a frown. Sarah had finally told him about what had happened in London. Could someone really have been following her? Might they have followed her all the way from London to the country?

Before he could continue his train of thought, Arthur was accosted by a strange looking man. Arthur stared at the man for a moment before he remembered... Jonas Pickering!

Jonas was dancing around in front of Arthur, shouting nonsense about the Four Towers, just as he had done on the previous day.

"Stay away! Stay away!" said the man, "You and your friend are bad for the Four Towers. You must keep away, lest you disturb things that are better left to rest!"

"What are you talking about?" said Arthur, crossly. This man was a nuisance. Was he going to keep bothering him and Sarah during their entire stay?

"There's evil there....beware Arthur and Sarah!" said the man, waving his arm in the direction of the Four Towers.

"What did you just say?" asked Arthur, shocked. How did this strange man know their names?

Suddenly curious, Arthur asked, "Why do we have to stay away from the Four Towers?"

Before Arthur could get Jonas to answer him, he heard his name being called from across the square. He turned to see Molly, Daniel, and Sarah, followed closely by Eustace, Margaret and another person whom Arthur didn't recognize.

Arthur waved to them and then turned back to where Jonas Pickering had been standing only a moment before, but the strange man was gone.

Daniel reached Arthur first, "Sorry you had to wait so long. It took longer than I wanted with Mrs. Bannerbee. I was on my way here when I ran into everyone else."

"That's okay," said Arthur, trying to compose his thoughts. He was feeling even more disturbed after his encounter with Jonas Pickering.

Arthur forced a smile. "It gave me more time to admire the quaint town square of the charming town of Castleton," he joked.

"That's good," laughed Molly, who had just reached the two. "I'm going to be showing you much more of this charming country town today. I thought I'd give you the grand tour and then we'd eat lunch at the Castleton Café. One of Caroline's friends owns it and it's really good."

"Sounds good to me," said Arthur. "As long as we get to eat, I'll be happy."

"I know," laughed Molly. "That's why I made sure I planned an early lunch for us today."

"I don't think we've all met," said Sarah, looking around the group assembled in the town square.

"Oh yeah," said Margaret, doing her best to avoid looking at Tad. "Daniel and Arthur, this is Tad," she muttered. "He's an intern with me this summer and we're working on a project together."

"So nice to meet you," said Daniel, shaking Tad by the hand.

"It's very nice to meet you Tad," said Arthur. "I give you a lot of credit. It must be a very scary experience working with Margaret."

"I've enjoyed it so far," said Tad, looking at Margaret and smiling.

Arthur and Daniel exchanged a questioning look. Was there something wrong with Tad? How could anyone enjoy working with Margaret?

Molly grinned mischievously at Daniel and Arthur. As soon as Margaret wasn't paying attention, she whispered, "Tad's completely in love with her!"

Arthur's eyes widened and he looked at Tad with new appreciation.

"Wow," he said. "He's a braver man than me!"

"How's the courtship going?" asked Daniel doubtfully.

"So far not very good for Tad," replied Molly, "but we're hoping we can help thaw her out a little during their visit."

"He's welcome to all of the help we can give him," said Arthur, "but I don't think he knows what he's getting into."

"What are the three of you whispering about over there?" said Margaret, in annoyance. "I don't like secrets. And, if we're going to be doing the whole tourist thing we need to get started. I have a lot of work to do this afternoon and I don't have time to be wandering around looking at stuff all day."

Molly, Arthur, and Daniel looked at Margaret and then at each other. "Thawing her out might be a harder task than anticipated!" Molly said, to the two boys. Then she walked over to Margaret and Tad and took them both by the arms.

"Alright," said Molly, "don't be impatient, we'll get going on our tour. You two can stay up here with me and get the star treatment."

With that, Molly proceeded to lead the way, with Eustace close at her heels, Daniel beside him, and Arthur and Sarah lagging a bit behind the others.

"I was hoping I'd get a chance to talk to you," said Arthur, in an undertone.

"Me too," said Sarah. "Sorry I wasn't able to make it into town earlier. I overslept this morning. And then Margaret and Eustace arrived and I couldn't get away."

"That's okay," said Arthur. "I didn't sleep well last night, so I wasn't up early either."

"Now that you mention it," said Sarah, "I think that's why I slept so late. I was having such weird dreams, but I can't remember them now."

"I was too," said Arthur, looking at Sarah more intently. "I think there might be something going on."

"With the Four Towers?" asked Sarah, quickly. "I was afraid of that."

"I was hoping it was nothing," said Arthur, "but I just don't feel right."

"I know," agreed Sarah. "There's something in the air today. It's making me nervous."

"It's either the Four Towers, or whatever you felt in London followed you down here," said Arthur. "But I think we need to get to the bottom of what's going on, before it gets any worse."

Sarah sighed and then said, "I don't think you're going to get that vacation you wanted."

Arthur smiled ruefully. "It doesn't look that way."

"Let's not give up yet," said Sarah. "We still have to talk to Uncle Alfred's friend. He might be able to explain some of what's been happening."

"An explanation would be nice," said Arthur. "I don't like feeling so worried."

"I don't either," said Sarah. "But we shouldn't have to wait too long. Molly's tour takes us right by the antique store that my uncle's friend owns. We can act like we found something we want to buy for my uncle and run into the store. We'll tell the others to go on without us. We can meet them for lunch later."

"You have it all planned out," said Arthur, appreciatively.

"Of course," said Sarah, with a smile. "You don't think that I'd come without a plan."

Arthur grimaced and looked at Sarah. "I just remembered something else that worries me."

"What else?" asked Sarah. "We already have enough to

worry about!"

"That weird man at the Four Towers yesterday..." began Arthur.

"Ugh," said Sarah. "Jonas Pickering! I hope I don't run into him anytime soon."

"Hopefully you won't," said Arthur. "But I just did. While I was waiting for everyone in the square he came up to me and started saying all sorts of wacky things."

"I can imagine," said Sarah. "I bet they're the same things he said to me yesterday."

"I tried to ask him some questions, but he just kept rambling, warning me to stay away from the Four Towers. And somehow he knew both of our names. It gave me the creeps!"

"That's strange," said Sarah. "How could he possibly know anything about us?"

"I don't know," replied Arthur. "But it definitely didn't give me a warm feeling."

The two paused in their conversation for a moment and looked ahead to where Molly and the others were waiting for them.

"Come on," said Molly, waving at the two stragglers, "you're missing all of the good stuff on my tour!"

Arthur and Sarah hurried forward, when suddenly Sarah stopped in her tracks. They were on a narrow street lined with small shops.

"Oh no!" said Sarah. She pointed at one of the shops on the street. It was dark and shuttered, clearly closed for the day.

"That's the store where my uncle said we'd find his friend," she said.

"Just our luck," said Arthur.

"Hopefully one more day won't make a difference," replied Sarah.

"Maybe," said Arthur, doubtfully. "But we definitely have to visit the store tomorrow."

"Sounds like a plan," said Sarah, as she and Arthur walked quickly towards Molly and the others.

"Have you developed an interest in antiques?" asked Molly, gesturing towards the shops, most of which were antique stores.

"Not for me," said Sarah. "But for my uncle. I want to buy him a present. One of the shops back there looked interesting, but it's not open today. Maybe I can come back tomorrow."

"Sure," said Molly. "My aunt can tell you the best places to check out. She's a bit of a nut for antiques."

Margaret groaned. "Can we stop talking about shopping? I don't have time for all of these delays."

"You heard Margaret," laughed Molly. "We need to get going, so no more delays! I have one more thing to show you, the medieval church, and then we're done with the grand tour."

"Thank goodness," moaned Eustace. "I'm starving! And all of this walking is making my feet hurt!"

"If you weren't wearing such ridiculous shoes your feet wouldn't hurt," said Margaret, unsympathetically.

"These shoes aren't ridiculous," protested Eustace. "Everyone's wearing them in Paris."

"Well you're not in Paris anymore," said Margaret. "Maybe you should wear what everyone is wearing here."

Eustace paused for a moment and looked around at everyone else's shoes. "That's a good idea!" he said, enthusiastically. "I could use some new clothes and shoes. Anyone want to go shopping with me after lunch?"

Margaret groaned, "Don't volunteer! Shopping with Eustace is a nightmare."

"I'll go with you," said Molly, kindly. "I can show you some of my favorite stores."

Eustace looked at Molly with dumb devotion. "You will?" he said, shocked speechless for a moment.

Then, with a huge smile, he continued, "I promise you won't regret it. Don't listen to what Margaret says. Shopping with me is fun!"

"Me and Tad are busy," said Margaret firmly, "so there's no

chance of us coming with you."

"That's okay," said Eustace, happily. "Molly and I will have a much better time without you around to spoil things."

"Now that we've cleared that up," said Molly, "let's look at the church and then off to lunch!"

*****

About an hour later, the friends were sitting around a large outside table at a small café, finishing the remains of a bountiful lunch.

"This is a nice place," said Tad to Molly. "Thank you for bringing us here."

"I'm so glad you like it. It's one of my favorite restaurants in town," answered Molly, happily. "It's small so not many people know about it. But the food is always wonderful."

"It certainly is," agreed Arthur. "Are you going to finish that?" he asked Sarah, pointing to some food left on her plate.

"No," she laughed. "And since you're obviously still starving, you can have it."

"Thanks," he said, grabbing her plate and stacking it on top of his.

"We're not leaving yet, are we?" asked Eustace, in alarm.

"Why?" asked Arthur.

"Because we haven't had dessert yet!" he answered. "I always have dessert with every meal. It's part of my training as a pastry chef. It's required...sort of like homework."

Margaret guffawed. "That's the stupidest thing I ever heard!" she said. "There's no reason you have to eat dessert. And anyway, Tad and I have to leave. I've wasted more than enough time today. Thanks for the tour Molly. And here's some money for lunch. That should cover everyone, even Eustace," she said, throwing a wad of bills on the table.

Margaret grabbed Tad's arm and yanked him from his chair.

"Bye everyone," he barely managed to say, before Margaret

pulled him away.

"Poor Tad," said Arthur, as soon as the two were out of earshot. "I wouldn't want to spend the afternoon with Margaret."

"Me neither," agreed Eustace promptly.

"I don't think we need to feel bad for Tad," said Sarah. "He likes spending time with her."

"It's too bad he doesn't have a chance," said Molly. "They'd make a nice couple."

"I don't know," said Sarah, thoughtfully. "Tad might have a better chance than we think. He just needs a little help."

"No more talk about Margaret!" whined Eustace. "It ruins my digestion and my appetite. We need to talk about more important things," he said, brandishing the dessert menu in front of them.

"I can help you pick," smiled Molly. "The desserts here are delicious."

A few moments later the two were immersed in the complexities of the dessert menu.

"I hope you have room for dessert," joked Arthur, looking at Daniel. "I think Molly and Eustace are going to order one of everything on the menu!"

Daniel made no reply. He was staring off into the distance, lost in thought.

"You've been awfully quiet today," said Arthur, observing at his friend more closely. "Is there something wrong?"

"No, nothing" said Daniel, with a start.

He paused for a moment and then said reluctantly, "Well, I guess I am a little worried about something."

"You!" said Sarah. "What could you be worried about?"

"Maybe it's nothing," said Daniel slowly. "But Mrs. Bannerbee had a window broken last night. That's why I was late this afternoon. I was helping her to fix it."

"A broken window doesn't seem that alarming," said Sarah.

"I'm not so sure," said Daniel. "Mrs. Bannerbee thinks it was just an accident, but I think someone was trying to break into the house. There've been other incidents in town... broken windows and doors, antiques and jewelry missing. But nobody seems to be taking it seriously. I don't think anything bad has ever happened in Castleton before."

"Anyway, I don't know what to do," continued Daniel. "There's a part time police force here, but I'm pretty sure they'd think I was crazy if I came to them with a story about some broken windows and lost jewelry."

"Maybe I can talk to Molly's uncle about it," said Sarah. "He might be able to help."

"Would you?" said Daniel, gratefully. "It would make me feel much better."

"I'll talk to him tonight," replied Sarah.

"Aright!" interrupted Eustace imperiously, "enough talking! Molly and I have made our decisions. I hope you have appetites adequate for the occasion. This is going to be a feast to remember!"

# CHAPTER VII
# NIGHTFALL

arah awoke with a start. A tremendous flash of lightning illuminated her room for a moment, followed by an alarmingly loud crash of thunder. The storm, which had been predicted for earlier that day, had finally come.

"It doesn't matter," muttered Sarah, who had been tossing and turning for the last few hours. "I wasn't sleeping anyway. Eating too many desserts doesn't lead to a good night's sleep!"

Sarah looked at the clock next to her bed. It was 2:00 AM.

"Ugh," she groaned. It was not a good time to be awake, but it was pointless to keep trying. She wasn't going to be able to sleep.

Sarah rolled herself out of bed and switched on a small lamp near her bed. "I guess I can read for a little while," she said to herself. "Sometimes that helps me to fall asleep."

Just then, there was a loud commotion in the yard outside.

"What could that be?" Sarah wondered. No one in their right mind would be outside on such a terrible night at such a late hour. What was going on?

Sarah padded downstairs and into the kitchen. From there, she opened the back door a crack and peeked out. She could see the figures of Molly's uncle Jacob and Jordan talking urgently in the back yard. They were both getting soaked.

Sarah poked her head out the door to hear what they were

saying.

"It's the sheep," said Jordan. "I heard a crash and came out. I think the gate to the pen was damaged and some of the sheep escaped. I secured the rest of them, but there are four missing."

Jacob looked grave. "I need to go after them," he said. "I can't leave them out on a night like this."

Jordan shook his head firmly, "We need to go after them. You can't do this alone."

"All right," Jacob replied. "I know I won't get very far arguing with you. Let's divide up. We'll each take one of the dogs. I'll head out towards the back field and you take the hill. We'll meet back here in an hour. Hopefully one of us will have found them by then."

Jordan nodded his head. He handed a flashlight to Molly's uncle and pulled his own from his raincoat pocket. In a few moments, the men had gotten the dogs from the barn and were on their way.

Sarah watched, wondering how anyone could go out on such a horrible night. Jordan took the path that led towards the hill and the Four Towers, his figure almost lost to sight due to the rain and fog.

Suddenly, Sarah's attention was caught by a flash of light coming from the direction of the Four Towers. She looked again, and there it was, a quick flash, followed by a blaze of light. There was evil and danger there, she could sense it quite clearly. And it was right where Jordan was headed.

Sarah ran back up to her room and threw some clothes on. She dreaded going out in the horrible weather, but she didn't have a choice. She had already seen what the Four Towers could do. She had to get there before Jordan did.

Sarah paused for a moment at the door to the house.

"Am I being crazy?" she asked herself, wondering if what she was doing made any sense.

Sarah glanced down at her ring. It was glowing dully in the darkness. The ring, which had never yet led her astray, confirmed her fears. She shook herself and pushed open the door.

"No," she said. "There's something wrong. I know it."

With that, she headed out into the darkness.

*****

Half an hour later, Sarah was at the crest of the hill that overlooked the Four Towers. She was wet through and through. The storm had gotten worse during her trek. The wind had picked up, lashing her with rain and whipping her breath away.

"Where is he?" she said, trying to peer into the darkness. Sarah had found a small flashlight in the kitchen before she left. But it didn't help to dispel the gloom that had gathered over the entire area. Every so often a flash of lightning illuminated her surroundings for a moment, before plunging her into darkness again.

Suddenly, Sarah saw a movement near the front of the castle. She was just able to make out something white and bedraggled emerging from the castle gate.

"One of the sheep!" she said. If the sheep were here, Jordan couldn't be that far off.

Just then, she heard a shout and saw the figure of Jordan emerge from the far side of the castle. He grabbed the sheep and secured it near the castle wall, leaving the sheep dog on guard. Then, he ran through the gate and into the castle grounds.

"The other sheep must be inside," said Sarah, as she began to make her way quickly, but cautiously, down the path.

Suddenly, another flash of lightning lit up the valley below. Sarah looked towards the castle ruins, and, to her horror, she could make out the ghostly shape of the fourth tower. It loomed out of the blackness at her, glowing with a sick yellowish light.

Sarah broke into a run. "Please don't let me be too late," she panted.

After what seemed like an eternity, Sarah reached the castle gate. She ran into the courtyard as quickly as she could. Ahead of her were the remaining sheep. They were on the far side of the courtyard, near the Fourth Tower, rooted to the spot in terror.

Caroline's story of the Fourth Tower and all of the strange happenings that had occurred at the site rushed through Sarah's mind. Caroline had said that the bodies of lost animals were sometimes found at the castle. It was believed that they died from fear.

Sarah tried to push these thoughts out of her head. "Find Jordan and get the sheep," she said to herself. "That's all I have to do."

Sarah's attention was suddenly attracted by another flash. This time it wasn't lightning. She looked towards the Fourth Tower. It had taken on a brighter glow and was flashing ominously in the gloom, as if warning her away.

Sarah shivered. Memories of her struggles at Westmere suddenly crowded in upon her. She felt the presence of a powerful evil here, just as she had at Westmere.

"Courage Sarah," she said to herself. "You can't stop now."

As Sarah reached the base of the Fourth Tower, a ring of flames shot out from the ground before her. Sarah fell back in fear, attempting to keep herself out of reach of the flames.

The flames shot up higher and higher, almost level with the top of the phantom tower. Suddenly, Sarah saw Jordan standing directly before her, right in front of the tower. Where had he come from? She hadn't seen him until just that moment. He was clearly in harm's way from the flames. Why didn't he run away?

As Sarah watched, she saw Jordan raise his arms towards the tower. It looked as if he was going to put his hands right into the flames. She had to stop him.

"Jordan!" she shouted, running frantically towards him. "Please stop!"

Jordan started, as if awakening from a deep sleep. He

stared at her unseeingly and then crumpled to the ground in a faint.

Sarah stood by his side protectively as the flames continued to surge around them. In a moment the two were surrounded by fire. She and Jordan would soon be engulfed if she didn't do something quickly.

Sarah closed her eyes and put out her hand. She summoned all of her powers, concentrating on the evil before her. Words, unbidden, rose to her lips. "Return to rest," she whispered.

Sarah struggled to control the flames. She was facing a powerful force. But, after a few moments, she could feel herself prevailing. Almost at once, the flames disappeared and the phantom tower faded slowly away. In a moment, nothing remained.

Sarah breathed a deep sigh of relief and then bent down over Jordan.

"Jordan," she said, kneeling on the ground beside him. "It's me, Sarah. Are you okay?"

Jordan opened his eyes and looked at Sarah uncertainly. "What are you doing here?" he asked weakly. "And what I am doing here?" he added, looking around in confusion.

"You don't remember?" she asked.

"No," he said. "I remember coming in here to get the sheep, and then there was a flash, it must have been lightning, and that's it."

Sarah thought for a moment. If Jordan didn't remember what had happened she didn't want to tell him. Plus, would he even believe her? Now that the tower was gone it all seemed so ridiculous.

"I couldn't sleep," explained Sarah. "When I saw you go after the sheep, I followed you. After hearing all of the stories about the Four Towers, I was afraid to let you come up here alone at night."

"At least that part of the story is true," Sarah thought to herself.

"You're crazy to be out on a night like this," said Jordan. "But I appreciate your help. I probably shouldn't have come up here by myself anyway."

"Let's try to get the sheep and get back to the house," continued Jordan. "I don't think this storm is over yet."

"The sheep were frozen when I came in," said Sarah. "I don't know if we're going to be able to move them."

"They get spooked by these storms," said Jordan, as Sarah helped him to his feet. "But usually I can get them to follow me."

The two walked over to where the sheep were huddled in the castle courtyard. They had not moved at all, completely immobilized by their own fear. Jordan squatted down next to the group. He began speaking in a soft, gentle voice, words that Sarah couldn't quite make out. And then, suddenly, the sheep began walking towards the castle entrance in an orderly line.

"Jacob said you had a way with animals. I think he was right!" said Sarah in amazement.

"If you hang around sheep enough, they'll do anything you want," said Jordan, with a tiny smile.

Sarah looked at him in surprise. This was the first time she had seen him so much as smile. Perhaps he had a bit of friendliness in him after all.

*****

As the two began their trek homewards, Sarah was lost in her own thoughts. What was going on at the Four Towers? She could feel the presence of evil and she had seen its manifestation twice. But what or who was the driving force behind it? She still had no idea.

Sarah sneaked a few glances at Jordan during their journey home. After a few moments of walking, it was as if he had forgotten she was with him. His face had taken on its normal closed, brooding expression, and he seemed oblivious to the world around him. The brief hint of friendliness that Sarah had observed in the castle ruins was gone.

Jordan was a mystery to her. There was something about him that made her nervous. And to make matters worse, he seemed to have an odd interest in her. According to Margaret, it wasn't a romantic interest...so what was it then? What could she possibly have to do with him? They were complete strangers.

Sarah's head was in a whirl. There were too many questions without answers. She could only hope that the next day's visit to Uncle Alfred's friend would shed some light on the mysteries she faced. Sarah knew that she needed to figure something out soon. The Fourth Tower wasn't going to wait for her before coming to life again.

Sarah was so lost in her own thoughts that the trip back to the house seemed extremely short. Before she knew it, she was standing in front of the door to the house with Jordan, the recovered sheep, and the dog.

"Jordan," said Sarah quickly, before entering the house, "if you could keep our little adventure to yourself I would really appreciate it. I probably shouldn't have followed you this evening."

Jordan nodded curtly his head and then walked off in the direction of the barn, animals trailing behind him.

Sarah shook her head. "At least I don't have to worry about him giving away my secret," she said to herself. "Maybe it's a good thing that he doesn't talk to anyone."

Sarah entered the house as quietly as she could and made her way to her bedroom where she changed into dry clothes. Luckily no one had seen her leave or enter the house. So she wouldn't have to make up a story regarding her whereabouts that evening. She couldn't imagine what Molly would make of her traveling up to the Four Towers in the middle of the night. It would be like Westmere all over again!

"I'm not going to be known as a witch here too," said Sarah to herself, as she dragged her weary body back into bed.

# CHAPTER VIII
# ANTIQUES

he next day, Sarah was in town bright and early. Arthur was already waiting for her at their meeting spot in the square.

"I'm so glad you're okay," Arthur said, in relief. "I couldn't sleep. I had a horrible dream about you and the Four Towers."

Sarah tried to smile, but failed. "I was at the Four Towers last night," she said.

Arthur frowned. "What were you doing there? I thought we agreed that we weren't going to go there unless we were together."

"I know," said Sarah. "I'm sorry. During the storm last night some of the sheep got loose. Jordan said he would go up to the Four Towers to look for them. I couldn't let him go alone. I didn't want anything bad to happen to him."

Arthur still looked unhappy. "Please don't do that again. Something horrible could have happened to both of you."

"I know," said Sarah, "but last night I didn't have a choice."

"I assume something bad did happen while you were there," said Arthur.

Sarah nodded. "It was so strange," she said, thinking back to the scenes of the previous evening. "When I got there, I could see the Fourth Tower, just like Caroline described! Jordan was standing right at the base of the tower, almost touching it. When I called out, he fainted and then flames and fire started shooting out of the tower. I was able to make things stop, but it didn't feel right. I wasn't the one in control of what was happening."

Arthur frowned again. "I don't like the sound of that. What about Jordan, was he okay?"

"He was fine," said Sarah, "just a little dazed. And he didn't remember anything that happened at the tower. He was almost friendly for a few minutes; he even smiled at me. But I only broke the ice temporarily. By the time we got back to the house we were complete strangers again.

"He's an odd one," said Arthur. "I don't really know what to make of him."

"I agree," said Sarah, thoughtfully. "He's just another mystery in this whole mess."

"But that's why we're here this morning," said Arthur, eagerly. "Maybe we'll be able to get one part of this mystery cleared up."

"You mean by talking to my uncle's friend?" asked Sarah. "I certainly hope so. We need someone who can give us answers, not more questions."

*****

A few moments later, Sarah and Arthur were standing inside Chen's Antiquities, the shop where they were supposed to find Tony Chen, the friend of Sarah's Uncle Alfred.

"Do you think we're in the right place?" whispered Arthur, as they stood in the doorway of the shop.

Both of them had expected to find an old, dusty antique store, stocked with strange curiosities and eccentricities. However, the store they had entered was new and modern. It was filled with very expensive antique furniture arranged in neat displays.

"He said Chen's Antiquities," said Sarah, doubtfully. "And that's what it said on the door. But this isn't what I expected."

Just then, a young Chinese man entered the store from the back. "Can I help you with something?" he asked, efficiently.

"Uh," said Sarah, not sure how to begin. "We're looking for a Mr. Chen."

"I'm Mr. Chen," said the man, looking at the two curiously.

Sarah and Arthur exchanged a glance. What was going on?

"Oh," said Sarah, at a loss. "We were expecting someone a little older."

The man looked at the two bewildered faces and laughed. "You must be looking for my father, Mr. Chen, Sr. He said there might be some people coming to see him."

Sarah looked at Arthur with relief. At least this wasn't another dead end.

"Sorry," she said, looking towards the younger Mr. Chen. "I didn't mean to be rude. Your father is a friend of my uncle's, and you seem much too young to be the person we were looking for."

"I'll take that as a compliment," said Mr. Chen. "And, now, if you just follow me to the back of the store, I'll introduce you to my father."

Mr. Chen led them through a small curtain that divided the front showroom from the back regions of the store. He took them through a narrow hallway, which opened into a small room. The room was lined with shelves that were overflowing with odd looking objects.

"You'll have to excuse the mess," said Mr. Chen. "I've managed to modernize the front of the store, but my father can't seem to get rid of this stuff. He says they're all treasures, but since no one ever wants to buy any of them, I don't understand why we keep them."

Sarah and Arthur looked around the room in wonder. They'd never seen anything quite like this collection before. It was incredible!

"Also," said Mr. Chen, leading them towards the back of the room, "my father is a bit deaf, so you'll have to make sure you speak loudly. And, just so you know, his English is excellent, but he'll pretend it's not when he's done talking to you."

The back of the room was dark and shadowy. Sarah and Arthur were almost in front of Mr. Chen's father before they realized it. He was a small man with a thick head of white hair and a deeply lined face. He looked like he could be at least a hundred years old. He was sleeping peacefully on a comfortable chair behind a small wooden desk.

"His afternoon nap," whispered the younger Mr. Chen.

"I hate to wake him," said Sarah. "We could come back."

"Oh no," replied his son. "It's fine. My father takes enough naps during the day for both of us. And, he'd be very upset if he knew he had visitors and I let them go. He doesn't get many visitors, especially visitors like the two of you."

Mr. Chen walked behind the desk to his father's side and touched him gently on the shoulder. The man's eyes snapped open, completely transforming his face. They were bright, eager, and alert, the eyes of a much younger man.

Mr. Chen whispered a few words to his father in Chinese and then looked at Sarah and Arthur.

"I'll leave you with him," he said, as he walked towards the front of the shop. "He's very excited to speak with you."

Sarah and Arthur approached the man before them slowly. Now that they were in his presence, they were a bit apprehensive. There was something about the old man that inspired awe. They felt as if they were in the presence of a king.

"Mr. Chen," said Arthur nervously, "thank you for seeing us. My name is Arthur and this is Sarah."

The old man stood up slowly and looked from Sarah and Arthur, and then back again. His gaze was deep and intense.

"Yes, yes," he said, "I see the family resemblance. Sarah, your uncle has told me much about you."

At that, Sarah looked surprised. The way her uncle talked about Mr. Chen she had assumed the two hadn't seen each other or spoken in some time.

"Don't be surprised," he said, reading her thoughts. "We

70

have ways of communicating that go beyond words. You should know that as a Guardian."

"And Arthur, the new discovery..." the man trailed off, looking at Arthur steadily.

"But you don't know, he hasn't told you yet," Mr. Chen mumbled softly to himself. "But you'll find out in time, all in good time."

Arthur listened curiously. What was the man talking about? Before he could ask, Mr. Chen had sunk back into his chair, and motioned Sarah and Arthur to take two chairs that were next to the desk.

"Now," said Mr. Chen, closing his eyes and settling into his seat. "What is it that I can help you with?"

"Well...." said Sarah. Now that she was in front of Mr. Chen, she wasn't sure how to begin. She didn't want him to think she was crazy.

"We'd like to know more about the Four Towers," said Arthur, finally.

"Ahhh, the Four Towers, the centerpiece of our little town...you've been there, I presume?" asked Mr. Chen, his dark eyes opening suddenly.

"Yes," said Sarah, "a few times now."

"And your visits haven't been that pleasant," said the man. "And you want to know why."

"I guess that's about it," said Arthur.

"Anything you could tell us would be very helpful," added Sarah.

"You've heard the legends, I suppose," said Mr. Chen, dreamily. "About crazy Montclair and his obsession...an obsession that led to his death, and the death of his wife."

"We have," said Sarah, "but we weren't sure how much of it was true."

"Right, right," nodded Mr. Chen, "it's always good to be a little skeptical."

"Do you know what Montclair was doing at the castle? Was he really involved in alchemy like people say?" asked Arthur.

"Alchemy," said Mr. Chen, musingly. "I suppose that's what people call it nowadays. But alchemy as it is understood today leaves much unsaid."

"What do you mean?" asked Sarah.

"Simple alchemy, transforming metals into gold, only touches the surface," replied Mr. Chen. "Real alchemy goes much farther. It reaches into deeper, darker realms."

Sarah shivered, even though the room wasn't cold. Something about what Mr. Chen was saying frightened her.

"Did Montclair get mixed up in real alchemy?" asked Arthur, curiously.

"Montclair didn't know what he was doing," said Mr. Chen, seriously. "He got in over his head, and it destroyed him. But that's what alchemy does to those who are not strong enough."

"What about the Philosopher's Stone?" asked Sarah. "Did he really find it? Or is that just a made up part of the legend?"

"The Philosopher's Stone is very real," said Mr. Chen, thoughtfully. "But again, our modern day understanding of the Philosopher's Stone is limited. Its power goes far beyond what most people can comprehend."

"What is it?" asked Arthur.

"It's hard to define exactly," replied Mr. Chen. "The alchemists thought it was the magical elixir or medicine that would make all things perfectly pure. It could purify any metal to gold. It could make sick people well by removing sickness. They even thought it could extend life. But most of the alchemists didn't understand that the Philosopher's Stone could do much more than that."

"Like what?" asked Sarah.

"The Philosopher's Stone isn't just able to purify things, it can also purify people. It turns people and makes them different. The perfect Philosopher's Stone gives the person who wields it power to make all things and people good, destroying evil completely."

"That sounds like a wonderful thing," said Sarah.

It would be," replied Mr. Chen, "if any of the alchemists

were truly successful. But they weren't. They kept trying and trying to make the Philosophers' Stone in their experiments. But they couldn't do it. That's because they didn't understand that creating such a substance requires generations and generations of work. It takes hundreds of years of time and dedication, the right ingredients, and the right people."

"So if none of the alchemists were able to make the stone, what did Montclair have?" asked Arthur.

"No one was ever completely successful in their pursuits," replied Mr. Chen. "However, one family of alchemists came close. They created the substance that Montclair accidentally came across many years later. A flawed version of the stone that was almost pure, but not quite."

"That doesn't sound good," said Arthur.

"It's not," replied Mr. Chen, gravely. "An impure stone still holds evil. It is extremely dangerous. It has almost all of the powers of the Philosopher's Stone, but instead of creating good, it spreads evil."

"So if Montclair had this evil stone," said Sarah slowly, "what happened to it? Did his wife destroy it when she jumped into the flames?"

"Ha!" said Mr. Chen. "You can't destroy the stone! You can only master it, or be destroyed by it yourself."

"However," continued Mr. Chen, "the stone can be put to rest. That's what Montclair's wife did. She wasn't swayed by the evil in the stone like her husband. Once the stone is put to rest, it is very resistant to being woken again. But, when it is awoken, it starts to look for a host, someone weak that it can turn to its own devices. The stone won't stop until it finds that person. The perfect person will be turned to evil, and then begin turning those around him. It's a process that is very hard to stop once it's started."-take out )

Sarah and Arthur exchanged a glance. This was much more than they had expected. Sarah felt as if her head was in a whirl. Were they really up against the evils that Mr. Chen was describing?

Suddenly, Mr. Chen stood up and began bustling about the room, evidently in search of something.

Sarah and Arthur watched him. It seemed impossible that he would be able to find anything in the accumulation of objects that filled the small room. But, almost magically, he knew right where to go in order to find what he was looking for.

"This might help you," said Mr. Chen. He held up a leather bound book, discolored and brittle from age. "This book explains some of the things you've been asking about."

He held the book out to Arthur. Arthur took it gingerly and held it in his lap, almost afraid it would disintegrate if he touched it.

"Read it well and carefully. As with anything to do with the stone, it won't give up its secrets easily," said Mr. Chen.

"And you," said Mr. Chen, looking intently at Sarah. "The stone has already reached out to you twice. It knows that you have power within you."

"How did you...." Sarah trailed off. She hadn't told him anything about what had happened to her at the Four Towers.

"Communicating without words," said Mr. Chen, with a small smile, "as I said before."

As he spoke, he held out a small piece of silver. It looked to Sarah like a broken piece of jewelry. She reached out and took it, holding it gently in her hand.

"A talisman," said Mr. Chen. "Perhaps it's nothing, but it's reputed to have been worn by Caroline, Montclair's ill-fated wife. She had the strength to put the stone to rest once. Her spirit may help you as well."

Sarah looked at the piece of jewelry more closely. It was half of a broken locket, shaped like a heart and deeply etched with intricate engraving.

"It's beautiful," said Sarah. "Thank you."

Mr. Chen settled himself behind the desk again, leaning back in his chair.

"But, I still don't understand everything," said Arthur.

"What are we supposed to do, just wait until the stone decides to do something?"

Mr. Chen looked at Arthur through half closed eyes. "Sorry," he said. "No understand. Talk to son."

With that, he closed his eyes firmly and was breathing peacefully in a few moments.

"Can we wake him up?" whispered Arthur. "I still have questions for him."

Sarah smiled. "I don't think it would make a difference. You heard his son. He only talks for as long as he feels like it."

"But, what are we supposed to do now?" said Arthur.

"Well," said Sarah slowly, "I think it's time for us both to do some reading. That book looks as if it holds the answers to our questions."

"I guess you're right," said Arthur, looking at the slumbering Mr. Chen in frustration. "But it would be much quicker if he just told us everything! Don't you think so?"

"Of course," said Sarah. "But if he just told us, that would take all of the fun out of everything!"

# CHAPTER IX
# ANOTHER CURIOUS BOOK

 t took a few moments for Sarah and Arthur to adjust to the bright sun in the street outside Chen's Antiquities. The backroom where they had met Mr. Chen had been dimly lit, and they were both dazzled by the sunshine.

"That's not who I think it is, is it?" asked Sarah, nervously, as she squinted and pointed down the road.

There, walking briskly towards them was Jonas Pickering. He was directly in their path and there was no way to avoid him.

"He finds us no matter where we are!" groaned Arthur.

Jonas Pickering was looking even stranger than normal. To his usual garb of mismatched, ill-fitting clothes, he had added several accessories. On his back was a tattered old rucksack, which looked as if it had originally been made centuries ago for an alpine climbing expedition. Two ragged, overstuffed messenger bags dangled from his shoulders. He looked like a wandering hobo who was extremely down on his luck.

"I knew I would find you here!" said Jonas, as soon as he reached them.

"You keep causing trouble," he continued, "first at the towers and now in town. Why don't you just let things alone? You aren't wanted here. Go back from whence you came! And avoid the towers! They're cursed!"

Jonas Pickering glared at them and began walking

backwards down the street, muttering the entire time.

"Danger, doom, darkness and despair for both of you. Beware of the Four Towers!"

"Ugh," said Sarah, as soon as he was gone. "How did we get mixed up with him?"

"I don't know," said Arthur, "but hopefully he's done with us for today. I don't think I can take any more Jonas Pickering!"

"Me neither," agreed Sarah.

"I know what I do need though, and that's lunch!" said Arthur, with a smile. "Let's get going. I promised Daniel we'd meet him at the café at noon. If we don't hurry we're going to be late."

*****

When Sarah and Arthur arrived at the café, Daniel was already there waiting for them. He smiled and stood up as they approached the table.

"I'm so glad you're here," said Daniel. "I was hoping we'd be able to talk today. Did you get a chance to talk to Molly's uncle?" he asked Sarah.

Sarah looked at him blankly for a moment, and then remembrance came flooding back. In all of the excitement of the previous evening she had forgotten about Daniel's request.

"Oh no!" she said. "I'm so sorry. I completely forgot. As soon as I get back this afternoon I'll talk to Jacob. I promise."

"It's okay," said Daniel. "I still think I might be overreacting. But what if there really is a thief and someone caught him in the act? I don't want anything bad to happen to anyone."

"You're right," said Arthur. "We should try to get to the bottom of this."

"Jacob is a good start," Arthur continued. "And, while Sarah is talking to him, how about you and I pay a visit to Mr. Chen, Jr.?"

78

"Who's that?" asked Daniel, curiously.

"Sarah and I were at his store this morning," replied Arthur. "It's an antique shop, with a lot of antique jewelry. If Mr. Chen's in the antique jewelry trade he might have heard about the robberies. He seemed pretty smart too. I don't think anything going on in town would get by him."

"That's a great idea," said Daniel, sounding relieved. "I really do appreciate your help. I was planning on trying to make Mrs. Bannerbee's house a little more secure this afternoon too. She's been so good to us. I want her to be safe."

"You're much too nice," smiled Arthur. "Mrs. Bannerbee is already devoted to you. And you've only been here a few days."

Daniel blushed. "I don't know what you're talking about. It's not as if I've done anything out of the ordinary."

Sarah laughed. "Your idea of ordinary is saintly to most people!"

"Anyway," said Arthur, "now that we have that figured out, can we please get something to eat? I'm starving!"

*****

Later that afternoon, Sarah and Arthur were ensconced in the parlor at Mrs. Bannerbee's house. They had decided to begin their study of the book Mr. Chen had given them.

"I only have about an hour before I have to go," said Sarah, "so we may not get very far today. Mr. Chen said the book wouldn't be easy to read."

"Of course not," joked Arthur. "We wouldn't want anything to be easy, would we?"

As Arthur spoke, he laid the book gently on the table in front of them.

"It looks ancient," said Sarah. "How old do you think it is?"

"Who knows!" said Arthur. "I'm almost afraid to open it. It looks so fragile."

"Unfortunately, I don't think we have a choice," said Sarah. "There's nothing on the cover that's going to help us."

There was no writing on the front or back cover of the book. Rather, it was decorated with an intricate scroll design deeply etched into the aged leather. It was damaged in spots, but still very beautiful to behold.

"Alright," said Arthur nervously, "keep your fingers crossed that this works."

Arthur slowly opened the book to the first page. There, before them, was a title page, which read:

Alchemy, the Philosopher's Stone, and Other Ancient Curiosities; herein being a description and explanation of the Mysteries and Magick attached thereto; with a further exposition on the Twelve Keys of the Ancient Alchemists, their meaning and practical application.

"That's a mouthful," said Sarah. "But it sounds promising. There must be answers to some of our questions."

Arthur turned slowly to the next page. It was a lengthy table of contents. Arthur moved his finger slowly down the page, reading the entries aloud.

*The Solution to the conundrums of distillation, calcination, and sublimation...page 3*

*Recipes of the Ancient Alchemists...page 35*

*The Mysterious Powder of Projection, its uses and dangers...page 89*

*The Philosopher's Stone, its history and secrets revealed...page 111*

Arthur stopped reading and said excitedly, "That sounds exactly like what we're looking for! Why did Mr. Chen make it sound like this book was going to be so hard to use?" he asked, as he flipped quickly to page 111.

When Arthur reached the page, he stopped for a moment in surprise. "This isn't what I thought it would be," he said in confusion.

Sarah and Arthur peered at the book before them. Rather than a chapter describing the Philosopher's Stone, as they had been led to expect, there was a strange etching of an outdoor scene, a garden filled with flowers and vegetables. Underneath the drawing was a caption, which read:

The time of year is where you'll find the secrets you desire.

"What does that mean?" asked Arthur. "That has nothing to do with the Philosopher's Stone! Maybe I got the page number wrong."

Arthur carefully turned the pages of the book back to the Table of Contents.

"The Philosopher's Stone; its history and secrets revealed," read Sarah, "page 46."

Next to the entry was a drawing of a person in dunce cap.

"What!" said Arthur. "It didn't say page 46 just a minute ago. And where did this picture come from?"

"I don't know," said Sarah. "But I think the book is trying to tell us that we did something wrong. Let's see what we find on page 46."

Arthur turned to page 46. As his eyes met the page, he sighed in frustration.

"Look at this," he said, "another dead end. How are we going to find out anything about the Philosopher's Stone if we can't even get to the right page?"

Arthur was ready to shut the book in frustration, when Sarah stopped him.

"Hold on," she said. "Let me look at this page for just a minute."

"Why?" said Arthur. "It's just another weird drawing like we saw on page 111, with the same stupid caption! It doesn't make any sense!"

"But it does," said Sarah slowly, as she looked more closely at the picture. "I think the book is giving us clues. It's like a game that we have to play. We figure out the clue and it will lead us to what we want to know."

Arthur groaned. "I hate games! Why can't we just have a normal book?"

"Look," said Sarah, "on this page there's a picture of spring flowers. And on the last page there was a picture of a garden. The caption said the time of year would help guide us. So the last picture was in the summer and this picture is in the spring."

"Yeah," said Arthur, "I get that. But I still don't see how that helps us. Spring, summer...what does it matter if we don't have a page number?"

"That's it!" said Sarah, excitedly. "The time of year is telling us the page number!"

"What do you mean?" asked Arthur.

"When's the first day of spring?" asked Sarah.

"Uh, I think it's in March," replied Arthur. "Maybe the 20th?"

"Alright," said Sarah. "So March is the third month, which gives us three. Combined with the 20th, that would be page 320. Let's try it. Turn to page 320 and see what we find."

Arthur looked at the drawing on the page before him again, understanding beginning to sink in.

"Maybe you're right," he said eagerly as he turned to page 320.

At the top of page 320 was the title: The Philosopher's Stone, its history and secrets revealed.

"We were right!" said Sarah, happily. "What a clever clue!"

Arthur rolled his eyes. "It may be clever, but I think it would be much easier to have a book that we could just read normally."

"We'll get there soon," said Sarah. "This book isn't going to give away its secrets easily. But that's probably a good thing. The book is trying to protect dangerous information."

"I guess you have a point," sighed Arthur. "So what does page 320 tell us?"

Sarah looked at the page before them and read slowly:

The stone must sleep and desires rest.

None with faint heart shall disturb its slumber.

The stone will only awake to one with much power.

"That's basically what Mr. Chen told us," she said thoughtfully.

"Right, said Arthur. "And we know that neither of us is trying to wake up the stone. So who's dumb enough to be disturbing it?"

"I don't know," said Sarah thoughtfully, "but let's keep going. I think we'll find out more if we can continue to decipher these clues."

Arthur groaned as he looked at the bottom of page 320. "That's all we get?" he said. "Three lines of information that we already know and another clue?"

"Don't complain," said Sarah, as she looked at the picture at the bottom of the page. "We know what we're doing now, so this second clue should be easier to figure out."

The picture on the page before them was of a celebration. There were people gathered in a large room bearing gifts.

"What does it mean?" asked Arthur.

"It looks like some kind of a party," said Sarah. She looked at the picture more closely. "And that person in the middle looks kind of like you," she added.

Arthur looked at the picture and shivered. "It does, doesn't it?" he said. "This book creeps me out."

"I think it's a birthday party," said Sarah. "When's your birthday?"

Arthur looked at Sarah and rolled his eyes. "How would the book know that?" he said. "It's January 26th, but I don't think that's going to help us."

"You'd be surprised," said Sarah. "This book knows more about us than we think."

"I agree," said Arthur. "But I can't imagine it would know about my birthday."

"Let's just see what's on page 126," said Sarah.

Arthur turned the pages of the book rapidly to page 126. He looked at the page and groaned. "I don't think I like this book anymore."

Sarah smiled at him. "But at least we got the clue right, no matter how strange it is."

She looked at the page before them and read,

The stone will meet intruders with anger.

It will not awake unless you have something to offer.

Find a host of uncommon weakness to give the stone.

It may be tempted to awake for you.

"That sounds bad," said Arthur. "I'd prefer a friendly stone to an angry one. And I don't like that part about the host."

"Me neither," agreed Sarah. "The stone is bad enough without some weak person it can control."

"But let's keep going," she continued. "I think we're on a roll. What's our next clue?"

Arthur looked at the picture on the bottom of the page. It was divided into four parts. "It looks like Castleton," said Arthur. "These are things that Molly showed us on her tour. Didn't Molly tell us Castleton was called the town of fours?"

"You're right," said Sarah, as she gazed more closely at the picture. "I'm surprised you remembered that. I didn't think you were paying attention."

"Of course I was," said Arthur. "I'm good at multitasking."

"Look," he continued, pointing at the picture, "here's the town square with the four main roads leading into it. Here are the four churches in town...this is the one that Molly showed us."

"And these are the four mountains that surround the town," continued Sarah. "And of course, here are the Four Towers."

"So are we supposed to turn to page 4?" asked Arthur.

"Hold on a minute," said Sarah. "What does the caption say?"

Arthur looked at the page and read.

Remember to add before proceeding.

"What does that mean?" asked Arthur.

Sarah was quiet for a moment as she looked at the page.

"Each picture is showing us four things," she said thoughtfully. "And the caption is telling us to add. So I think we're supposed to add up the fours, which gives us 16. Should we try page 16?"

"Sure," said Arthur, rubbing his head. "All of this is making my head hurt though."

Arthur turned the pages of the book slowly to page 16. This time there were only words and no pictures or additional clues.

"No more clues," said Arthur. "Do you think this means the book is done with us, at least for now?"

"There's only one way to be sure," said Sarah. She thumbed through a few pages of the book, going forward and back from page 16. They were all blank.

"Yes," said Sarah. "I think it's safe to say the book is done with us for today. So this is our final piece of information," she said, as she looked at page 16.

Sarah read aloud slowly,

The awakened stone will do what it wills.

The pursuit of gold is a waste of the stone's powers.

The stone seeks to spread evil using the weak.

Few are those who are strong enough to control the stone.

Beware of the Philosopher's Stone!

It is best to be avoided.

"That's cheerful," said Arthur. "It sounds like a warning from Jonas Pickering. But maybe the book has a point. Avoiding the stone seems like a good idea to me."

"It's too late now," said Sarah. "Someone already woke it up."

"But who?" said Arthur. "And how do we turn the stone off?"

"I'm not sure," said Sarah slowly. "But I think this book still holds a few secrets. Let's hold onto it a little longer. I think it will tell us everything we want to know. We just need to be patient."

"That's fine with me," said Arthur. "But you can keep the book. I don't want it around. I don't think it likes me."

Sarah smiled. "Alright," she said. "I'll keep working on the book. But that means it's your job to figure out who woke up the stone."

Arthur smiled and said, "Sounds like a deal. I think I already have an idea of who it might be."

"Who?" asked Sarah, curiously.

"What do you think about Jonas Pickering?" asked Arthur.

"Jonas Pickering!" said Sarah. "I think he's crazy!"

"Think about it for a minute," said Arthur.

Sarah paused, turning the idea over in her mind. "I guess it's possible," she said finally. "But wouldn't we have sensed something from him...some feeling of evil?"

"Not necessarily," said Arthur. "Remember what we learned at Westmere. People can mask their powers. Neither of us had any idea that Morlock was behind everything."

"That's true," said Sarah.

"And," continued Arthur, "Jonas Pickering has been trying to scare us and just about everyone else away from the Four Towers. If he knew about the stone and was trying to use it then he wouldn't want people disturbing him, right?"

"Right," said Sarah. "You have a point. But he seems like such an unlikely person!"

"I know," said Arthur. "But I don't think we can discount him just yet. I'm going to follow him around for a little while. I'll try to see what he's up to without him knowing that I'm there."

"I hope your following skills have gotten better," Sarah said, with a smile. "Do you remember how bad you were at it when you tried to follow me that first time at Westmere? It sounded like I was being followed by a herd of elephants!"

"I'm much improved," laughed Arthur. "You don't become a Guardian without picking up a few skills on the way. I'm actually looking forward to following Jonas Pickering. He's been annoying both of us since we got here. Even if he's not behind the trouble at the Four Towers, I still want to know what he's up to."

86

"I agree," said Sarah. "And while you're doing that, I'll continue working on the book. Ideally, I'd like to know how to put the stone to rest before our next visit to the Four Towers. At the very least it would be nice to know how to calm it down."

"That would be nice," agreed Arthur. "A less agitated stone would be much easier to deal with!"

"Oh," said Sarah, suddenly remembering something else. "What about Daniel? We promised that we'd help him too!"

"Right," said Arthur, "I almost forgot again. Daniel and I can talk to Mr. Chen tomorrow. And you can talk to Molly's aunt and uncle tonight."

"That's perfect," said Sarah. "I'd like to get a little more information from Caroline about the legend of the Four Towers anyway. There's something about it that's bothering me, but I can't figure out what it is."

"Alright," said Arthur. "We both have our assignments. Let's spend some time investigating. Hopefully within the next few days we'll be ready to take another excursion out to the Four Towers, just the two of us."

"It sounds romantic when you put it that way," laughed Sarah.

Arthur grimaced. "Unfortunately I don't think there's anything romantic about the Four Towers!"

# CHAPTER X
# MATCHMAKING

hy do you always have to make such as mess?" scowled Margaret. "I don't understand why you can't cook like a civilized person!"

"For your information," replied Eustace haughtily, "I'm not cooking, I'm baking. There's a big difference. And I have to make a mess. It's part of the process. Baking is an art form."

"Whatever you say," muttered Margaret. "But don't expect me to help you clean up this disaster!"

A day had passed since Sarah and Arthur's experience with the book Mr. Chen gave them. Sarah had been trying to work on deciphering more of the book's secrets, but she was finding the task very difficult. In addition to the challenges of the book itself, there was also the distraction from the kitchen. Sarah was sitting in the parlor that adjoined the kitchen and Margaret and Eustace were extremely noisy.

The two had come over that afternoon so that Eustace could practice his baking. He was planning a large dessert-themed dinner party that coming Sunday. Margaret and Eustace were going to be heading back to France a few days later, and Eustace wanted to do something to celebrate the end of their visit.

Sarah sighed and pushed the book away from her. She wasn't going to accomplish anything more that day. But having a break would be good for her. She had been working too hard over the past few days, without much to show for her efforts. Some time spent with her friends would be a helpful diversion.

Sarah poked her head into the kitchen, where she saw a flour-covered Eustace with Margaret towering imperiously over him.

"Where's everyone else?" asked Sarah, unable to keep from smiling at the scene that met her eyes.

"I think they're outside, communing with nature," said Margaret, "or something horrible like that. Molly said something about harvesting. It sounded like it involved dirt, so I decided to stay here. Not that here is all that much better," she added, with a critical glance around the kitchen.

"Hey!" protested Eustace, who was retrieving a large tray of cream puffs from the oven. "You shouldn't complain. You've sampled just about everything I've made so far."

"I'm helping with quality control," said Margaret, in a dignified tone. "Really Eustace, I don't see how you can expect to turn out a good product if you don't have a quality control process in place."

"I'm quite capable of quality control myself," said Eustace, as he gobbled down one of the warm cream puffs.

"Your palate isn't refined enough," scoffed Margaret. "You need someone with a little more sophistication, an epicure like myself, for instance."

"Would you like one?" Eustace asked Sarah, ignoring his sister. "They're really very good."

"No thanks," said Sarah. "But I might try one later. I'm going to go look for everyone else. Maybe I can help them with the harvesting."

"I think it's safer to stay here," said Margaret, "but suit yourself."

"I'll take my chances with the dirt," answered Sarah, with a smile.

Sarah left the kitchen through the back door of the farmhouse. As always, the sight that met her eyes was breathtaking. It was another lovely summer day, pleasant and sunny, with a light breeze. The forecast predicted storms later that evening, but at the moment the weather was beautiful.

Sarah breathed in deeply. Hopefully some time outdoors would help clear her head. She felt as if she was right on the verge of some important discovery regarding the Four Towers, but it just wouldn't come to her. A break spent outside was just what she needed.

Sarah walked through the back gate onto a path that ran behind the house. She could see a group of people ahead of her, working in one of the fields. It must be Molly and the rest of her friends. Arthur, Daniel, and Tad had all come out for the day to help Jacob and Caroline with the summer harvesting.

Sarah began walking towards her friends, taking a path that skirted the edge of the fields. The path was one of her favorites. It curved and twisted around the fields, passing in and out of the woods bordering the farmland. Sarah always found it very peaceful. After the stress of the last few days, it was nice to feel a little more relaxed.

Sarah was walking slowly around a sharp curve in the path, lost in pleasant reveries. As she turned the bend, sunlight filtering through the trees almost blinded her. She looked up, and there, outlined darkly against the sun, was a towering figure of man holding up his arm, ready to strike at her. Sarah felt the same dread grip her that she had felt on her last day in London. For a moment, she was frozen in fear. Then she began to move away quickly, trying to get away from the horrible apparition. In her haste, her foot caught on a tree root and she stumbled and almost fell.

As she tried to right herself, Sarah felt a hand on her arm, steadying her. She almost screamed, thinking it was the man she had seen, but when looked up, all she saw was the reassuring figure of Jordan.

"Are you okay?" he asked in concern. "You looked like you were about to fall. These old paths can be a bit dangerous, lots of exposed roots and broken tree branches to trip people up."

Sarah didn't know what to say. Were her eyes playing tricks on her? She was almost sure she had seen a terrifying figure on the path before her. But now there was nothing, just Jordan.

"I thought I saw something in the trees ahead," said Sarah, "it startled me and I almost tripped."

"There are all sorts of wild animals in these woods," replied Jordan. "They scare me sometimes too."

Jordan looked at her for a moment, an intense, unsettling gaze. After a moment, he looked away, his momentary interest in her seemingly gone. Then, without another word, he turned away and walked down the path.

"What is it about Jordan?" she said musingly, as she watched his retreating figure striding quickly back towards the house. "I feel like he's mixed up in all of this too, somehow."

Before Sarah had time to ponder the matter further, she was hailed by Molly's Uncle Jacob, who was leading the group of harvesters.

"You finally came to join us!" he said. "Don't worry. We saved all of the hard work for you."

Sarah smiled. She doubted there was much work to do at all. Jacob and Jordan had been out in the fields early that morning. Most of the real work was probably already done.

"Good," said Sarah. "That's what I came for," she smiled.

"Alright," he replied. "You heard the girl! I think we should all take a break while we put her to work."

*****

A few hours later, Sarah and her friends were heading back towards the house, weary but happy after a successful day of harvesting. Sarah found herself walking next to Tad, who she hadn't seen in the last few days. Poor Tad! Margaret was certainly keeping him busy.

"I'm glad you were able to join us today," said Sarah. "It was nice of Margaret to let you have the time off."

Tad smiled a bit ruefully. "She's a very hard worker," he

said, "but she does get things done."

"You don't have to tell me," agreed Sarah. "I've seen her in action firsthand."

Sarah shuddered as she thought about her initial encounters with Margaret at Westmere Academy. Back then, Margaret had been out to ruin Sarah's life. Luckily, they had ended up becoming allies, and then friends, or at least as close as Margaret got to having friends.

"How are you two getting along?" asked Sarah curiously.

"Okay, I guess," sighed Tad. "I don't think Margaret thinks of me as much more than a tool she can use to get things done...or an inconvenience if I don't go along with her plans."

"That's Margaret for you," said Sarah. "She's very driven."

Tad smiled. "That's one way to put it."

He paused for a moment, and then took a deep breath and plunged in, "But how do I get her to notice me? I mean, really notice me?"

Tad's face had reddened and he looked embarrassed.

"You mean as a friend?" asked Sarah.

"Yes," replied Tad, "And maybe a little more than just a friend.

"I thought you might be leaning that way," smiled Sarah. "I was hoping we'd get a chance to talk. There are a few things you need to know about Margaret. First of all, she doesn't generally have boyfriends unless she can use them for some practical purpose."

"I've noticed," said Tad. "I've tried everything I can think of, but there doesn't seem to be a way to get to her heart."

"That might be impossible," said Sarah. But you can reach her in other ways."

"How?" asked Tad, sounding desperate. "I'm beginning to give up hope."

"Don't give up just yet," said Sarah. "You haven't tried the best approach. You need to go after her practical, business side and impress her. If she thinks you're stronger and tougher than her, you'll have done all that you need to do."

Tad thought for a few moments. "I've been going about it all wrong!" he said. "I thought being thoughtful and kind would win Margaret."

"Definitely not," said Sarah.

"I think I know what to do," said Tad, excitedly. "I just hope it's not too late! She probably despises me by now."

"If you come on strong enough, you'll turn the situation around, I promise," said Sarah. "If there's one thing that Margaret respects it's a person who takes charge and gets what he wants."

Tad smiled. "I can do that," he said. "Watch and wait. Hopefully in a few days I'll have turned the tables on Margaret Pritchard!"

# CHAPTER XI
# LOCAL CONCERNS

he next day, Sarah forced herself to get up early. She wanted to be at breakfast when Jacob and Caroline arose and before Jacob left the house. Since they were very early risers, it was quite a task. But Sarah still hadn't been able to fulfill her promise to Daniel regarding the robberies in town. There had been so much going on over the last few days and Jacob had been so busy on the farm that she hadn't been able to question him. This morning might be her only chance, and she didn't want to miss it.

"Well you're up awfully early," said Jacob, when Sarah poked her head into the kitchen.

"Do you mind if I join you?" she asked.

"Not at all," replied Caroline. "It's actually nice to have some company this early in the morning. Usually it's just the two of us."

"Don't say that like it's a bad thing," said Jacob playfully. "Isn't my company good enough for you?"

"Of course it is," smiled Caroline, "you know I love our time together in the morning. But a little variety is always nice."

"And what wakes you so early today?" asked Jacob. "Nothing bothering you I hope?"

"I'm not sure," said Sarah. "I couldn't sleep. I was thinking about something Daniel noticed in town. Have either of you heard anything about robberies?"

"Robberies!" said Caroline, in surprise. "Not in Castleton! Nothing bad ever happens here."

Jacob's brow furrowed and he looked at Sarah with interest. "Why do you ask?"

"Daniel's been worried for the past few days," explained Sarah. "Your friend, Mrs. Bannerbee, where Daniel and Arthur are staying, had a window broken and a few pieces of jewelry go missing. And some other people in town have had similar things happen. Daniel was concerned, but no one's taking it seriously. He doesn't know what to do."

"I've heard some rumors," said Jacob, slowly, "but I wasn't sure what to think."

"You didn't tell me!" said Caroline to Jacob. "How can this be possible? I don't think there's ever been a robbery in Castleton before. We don't even have a real police force!"

"Do you think there might be some truth to Daniel's suspicions?" asked Sarah.

"I do," said Jacob, seriously. "And I have my own suspicions about who might be behind the robberies."

Caroline looked at her husband. "Why didn't you tell me any of this before? And who do you think is behind these so-called robberies?"

Jacob smiled at Caroline's questions. "I'm sorry dear," he said. "I didn't want to alarm you. And I wasn't all that sure myself. But from what Sarah says, I'm not the only one who's noticed that there's something not quite right in Castleton."

"So if there is something going on," said Caroline impatiently, "who do you think is behind it?"

Jacob paused for a moment and sighed, "Jonas Pickering," he said.

Caroline and Sarah looked at each other in surprise.

"But he's crazy!" said Caroline. "He can barely complete a sentence. I doubt he could be behind a robbery!"

Caroline turned towards Sarah. "What do you think Sarah?" she asked. "You've had several unpleasant encounters with him. Do you think he could be a successful robber?"

Sarah shook her head slowly. "I don't know. He's so strange and frightening. He just seems crazy to me."

Jacob sighed again and said, "He wasn't always crazy. In fact, until a few years ago, he was just as normal as we are. We used to be friends."

"You were friends with Jonas Pickering!" said Sarah in surprise.

"We were close friends for many years," replied Jacob. "He's a local through and through, just like Caroline. His family has lived in Castleton for generations. He used to be a doctor... he moved up to London and had a nice practice there for many years. But then something went wrong. When he came back to town a few years ago, he was the way he is now. No one really knows what happened to him. Supposedly he's living in an old, rundown cottage on the outskirts of town, but, as you know, he spends most of his time out at the Four Towers. "

"Why do you think he's behind the robberies?" asked Sarah, curiously.

"Just a hunch," said Jacob slowly. "I don't believe that he's as crazy as he acts. And, the last time I was up in London, I ran into an old friend. He also knows Jonas and told me some strange stories about him. Jonas was making outlandish claims about how rich he was going to be soon. When I heard the rumors about the robberies in town, I put two and two together and came up with Jonas."

"That's not much evidence to go on," said Caroline, skeptically. "It's all feelings and stories, no real facts."

Jacob smiled. "And that's why I didn't say anything to you, dear. I knew you wouldn't believe me!"

It's not that I don't believe you," replied Caroline. "I just find it hard to believe that crazy Jonas Pickering could be capable of anything besides frightening people away from the Four Towers!"

"And why is he so obsessed with the Four Towers?" mused Sarah. "If he's not crazy, like you think, then there must be some other reason that he's scaring people away."

"I'm not sure what that's all about," said Jacob. "But his obsession, as you call it, has become a local nuisance. For years, people in town have wanted to raise enough money to restore the Four Towers to its rightful state and make it a real attraction for people visiting the area. Right now we get a few visitors, but there would be many more if the site was restored. But Jonas has spoiled all that."

"I wish we knew what the connection was," said Sarah. "If Jonas is the robber, there must be something about the Four Towers that's important to his plan."

Jacob smiled at Sarah. "You sound like a detective! But I think you need to let me worry about Jonas. I'm keeping an eye on him. And for now, I think you'd better stay away from him and the Four Towers, just in case."

Sarah nodded, feigning agreement. Of course she couldn't avoid the Four Towers or Jonas! But she didn't have to let Jacob and Caroline know that.

"Good," said Jacob. "Now that we've settled that, let's say we get going on these pancakes. I don't think they're going to last long once everyone else is up and I want to make sure we get our fair share."

"Sounds good to me, replied Sarah with a smile. She didn't like getting up so early, but so far her morning had been very productive. She had information that would reassure Daniel and she had found out more than she had bargained for regarding Jonas Pickering. She couldn't wait to talk to Arthur. If only her afternoon could be just as productive she'd be very happy. She had a date with Mr. Chen's mysterious book. She was hoping it would finally divulge its secrets!

*****

Arthur felt more relaxed than he had in several days. It had been nice to take a break from the Four Towers and spend some time with his friends. However, this morning he had to get back to work. He planned to visit Mr. Chen's store and spy on Jonas Pickering and he wanted to get an early start.

Arthur was happy to see Daniel waiting for him when he got downstairs.

"You're up earlier than me," said Arthur.

"I wanted to make sure I didn't miss you," replied Daniel. "I didn't want you sneaking off without me."

Arthur smiled. "No chance of that this morning," said Arthur. "I'm actually glad to have some company for a change."

Mrs. Bannerbee's house wasn't very far from Castleton's shopping district. After only a few moments of walking, Daniel and Arthur reached the street where all of the antique shops were located. Arthur led the way to Mr. Chen's store, which was located at the far end of the street. He was hoping the store would be open at such an early hour.

As soon as he could make out Mr. Chen's store, Arthur breathed a sigh of relief. The shop was clearly open. In fact, Mr. Chen, the younger, was standing outside the door, almost as if he was waiting for their arrival.

"Did he know we were coming?" asked Daniel.

Before Arthur could answer his friend's question, Mr. Chen hailed them from across the street.

"How are you, Arthur?" he said.

Arthur was surprised that the younger Mr. Chen remembered his name. They had only spoken for a few moments.

"And Daniel," he continued. "It's nice you came along too."

"How did he know my name?" whispered Daniel.

Arthur shrugged. "I have no idea," he replied.

"Hi Mr. Chen," said Arthur, as he and Daniel approached the store.

"You have something you want to ask me about," said Mr. Chen, looking curiously at the two.

Arthur wondered how much Mr. Chen already knew. Just like his father, the younger Mr. Chen seemed to know everything.

"We actually do," said Arthur. "I hope you don't mind."

"Not at all," replied Mr. Chen. "I'd like to help you, if I can."

"Thank you," said Arthur, not sure how to begin. "We were wondering if you'd heard anything about robberies in town, specifically antique jewelry."

"Hmmmm," said Mr. Chen. "And why are you worried about stolen jewelry?"

"It's actually more of a worry of mine," said Daniel. "We're staying with Mrs. Bannerbee in town...perhaps you know her?"

"Of course," replied Mr. Chen, "everyone knows Mrs. Bannerbee."

"Well," continued Daniel, "she's noticed a few things of her own that have gone missing over the past few weeks. Several of her friends have had similar experiences. Also, it looks like there was an attempt to break into her house just a few days ago. I'm very worried, but no one is taking it seriously. I had Mrs. Bannerbee talk to the local police force, but they don't believe anything bad could ever happen in Castleton."

"The police," Mr. Chen laughed, "I don't think I'd even call them real police!" he said. "They're not at that level."

"I hope you don't think we're being crazy," said Daniel. "It's just that I feel like something isn't right, and I don't know what to do about it."

"No," said Mr. Chen slowly, "I don't think you're crazy. I actually think you're a very perceptive young man. And I think you came to the right person with your concerns."

"We did?" said Daniel, in surprise.

"Is there something you know?" asked Arthur.

"I wouldn't say anything definite," replied Mr. Chen, "but, as an antiques dealer, I keep a close eye on the market. Antique jewelry is one of my specialties. I've noticed a few odd disappearances myself. And I've also noticed some interesting antiques showing up in town mysteriously."

"You have?" said Daniel. "Then there really is something going on!"

"Now let's not get ahead of ourselves," said Mr. Chen. "We

need to be cautious until we have definite proof. I've been watching my neighbor, Mr. Silverstone, in the Castleton Antiques Shoppe very closely. If there is anything going on, I'm pretty sure he's involved in it."

Arthur and Daniel both looked down the road. The store to which Mr. Chen had alluded was located on the corner of the street. Arthur almost gasped. It was the very spot where he and Sarah had been accosted by Jonas Pickering just a few days before.

Before he could stop himself, Arthur burst out, "You don't think that Jonas Pickering is mixed up in all of this too, do you?"

Mr. Chen glanced sharply at Arthur. "You're a better detective than I am!" he said. "I'm not positive, but I have my suspicions. I've noticed him hanging around Mr. Silverstone's shop quite often lately. I'm beginning to think they're involved in something together."

"So what are we supposed to do?" asked Daniel. "We're all agreed that there's something strange going on, but how can we stop it?"

"You leave that to me," said Mr. Chen. "I have eyes and ears all over this town. And come back tomorrow...I might have more information to share with you by then. In the meantime, try not to worry too much. And I'd suggest that you avoid Jonas Pickering. I don't want either of you to get involved in anything that could be dangerous.""

Arthur nodded, apparently agreeing with him. "Thank you Mr. Chen," he said. "We appreciate you taking the time to talk with us."

"You're welcome. I'll see the two of you tomorrow," replied Mr. Chen, as he went back into his shop, leaving Arthur and Daniel standing in front of his store.

"Are you really going to avoid Jonas Pickering?" asked Daniel, doubtfully.

Arthur smiled. "No," he replied. "But I didn't want Mr. Chen to know my plans."

"Do you want me to come with you?" asked Daniel.

"Sorry," said Arthur, "I think this part of the project is a one-man job."

"I see," said Daniel. "I don't like the idea of you going alone, but for some reason I'm not worried. After what you did at Westmere, I'd trust you with anything."

"Anyway," continued Daniel. "Molly's coming by later this afternoon, and I also promised Mrs. Bannerbee that I'd help her with a few things around the house. Plus today is Mrs. Bannerbee's cookie baking day, so I definitely don't want to miss that."

"Just my luck," said Arthur. "Try to save a few for me!"

# CHAPTER XII
# DETAILS EMERGE

fter Daniel left, Arthur took up his position at the end of the street. From there, he had a perfect view of Mr. Silverstone's store. Arthur had a hunch that Jonas Pickering was going to make his appearance; he just wasn't sure when.

Arthur settled in for a long wait. He would have to try to be patient, not one of his strong suits. But the wait would give him some time to think. And he definitely needed it! So much had changed in such a short space of time. Before he had met Sarah, he was a different person. Finding out that he was a Guardian and then all of the incredible things that had happened at Westmere Academy...it was still hard for him to believe!

Arthur had learned a lot about the Guardians during the time he had spent traveling with Alfred that summer. They had roamed all over the place, meeting other Guardians and learning from them. It had been an incredible time. Arthur felt as if he had soaked up vast amounts of knowledge and power from the people he had met.

But it had also been tiring. Arthur had been hoping for a real vacation in England. He hadn't counted on the Four Towers and dealing with another mystery. But perhaps it was for the best. He was getting a chance to use his skills, or as Alfred kept saying, remember his skills.

A loud shout suddenly broke into Arthur's thoughts.

"I'm coming, I'm coming," heard Arthur. When he looked up, he saw Jonas Pickering headed towards Mr. Silverstone's antique store. There was no one with him, but that didn't surprise Arthur. He was used to Jonas Pickering muttering and talking to himself.

Arthur thanked his luck and then stepped carefully forward. As he did so, he focused all of his thoughts on remaining undetected by Jonas Pickering. Suddenly, he could feel himself blending into the landscape around him. It wasn't as if he was invisible. But he knew he wouldn't be noticed.

Alright, alright," muttered Jonas to himself. "I'll get there. Stop rushing me! You know I don't like to be rushed."

Arthur wondered yet again if Jonas was really crazy. He certainly gave every indication of it. Yet, there was something about him that didn't add up. Arthur hoped Sarah had been able to find out more about him. It might help all of this make sense.

Instead of heading into the store, Jonas turned away from the front door and walked down an alleyway that bordered one side of the shop. Arthur followed cautiously, keeping at a safe distance.

When Jonas reached the back of the shop, he walked up to a large door and proceeded to pound on it.

"I'm here!" he shouted, as he continued banging. "I'm ready for lunch!"

Arthur felt a pang of disappointment. Was Jonas really only there to get food from Mr. Silverstone? It didn't seem possible.

Arthur moved a bit closer. As he did so, Mr. Silverstone stuck his head out the back door and said loudly, "Hold your horses! It's coming. You don't have to be so impatient!"

Mr. Silverstone disappeared for a moment and then reappeared, holding a large bag in his hand, filled to the brim with food for Jonas Pickering. But, just as Jonas was about to take the bag, Mr. Silverstone grabbed a well wrapped object from inside the store and surreptitiously put it into the bag.

Arthur could just hear Mr. Silverstone's harsh whisper.

"It's all there," he hissed. "Make sure you get it out of here today. I've got people breathing down my neck and I don't want anything found in the shop. You know where to put it. It needs to be there by nightfall. It'll be taken from there tonight."

Arthur was shocked at what he was hearing. Mr. Chen was right! Jonas Pickering and Mr. Silverstone were working together. Arthur wasn't sure what they were up to, but it had to be something underhanded.

Jonas Pickering acted as if he hadn't heard Mr. Silverstone, but Arthur saw him give the man a large wink. Then he said, "Thank you, thank you from the bottom of my heart I thank you. Some people in this town want me to starve, but not you. You are a good and generous man!"

As Jonas spoke, he backed away from the store and made his way out to the street again. Arthur followed him warily. He'd have to keep his guard up now. Jonas Pickering was definitely more than he seemed.

As Arthur reached the street, he could hear Jonas muttering, "Off to the Four Towers....off to the Four Towers..."

"It all leads back to the Four Towers," said Arthur to himself. "That's where I need to go."

\*\*\*\*\*

Sarah was sitting upstairs in her room, working diligently with Mr. Chen's book. She'd started at least an hour ago, but so far she hadn't made any progress. The book, which had been so cooperative at first, was now closed to her. She didn't understand it. Nothing had changed. Why wouldn't the book help her anymore?

Sarah closed the book again, starting over for yet the hundredth time. She opened to the Table of Contents and found the section she wanted on the Philosopher's Stone.

"This time it's page 50," she muttered to herself in

frustration.

Every time Sarah opened the book there was a new page number listed in the Table of Contents. But, no matter what page she turned to, the book wouldn't give her any new information or clues. There were no riddles to decipher or hints about what she should do next. She just kept finding dead ends.

"Let's see what I get this time," said Sarah, slowly turning to page 50.

She groaned as she saw what was on the page. She kept coming up with nothing! It was almost the same illustration that she had seen last time. The book just kept repeating itself, over and over again. Each illustration was a variation on the same theme, two people exchanging gifts.

Sarah was getting frustrated. She didn't know what the book was trying to tell her.

"What am I supposed to get from this?" she muttered in exasperation. "Is it Christmas or a birthday party? What? I don't understand."

Sarah was ready to give up. She sighed, resting her head in her hands. As she did so, strains of music could be heard from the downstairs parlor. Sarah smiled slightly. Molly must be practicing the piano. Molly played exquisitely and Sarah always loved listening to her. She closed her eyes for a moment, soaking in the music.

Sarah's rest was interrupted by a flash of light from the book. She gasped. What was the book doing? As she watched, the picture of the two people exchanging gifts flashed more brightly, almost in time to the music that Molly was playing. Then, suddenly, a number appeared at the bottom of the page. Could it be? Was this the clue that Sarah had been waiting for?

Sarah turned rapidly to the page number indicated. There, she saw a page covered with writing. This was it! Here was the information she needed. Sarah didn't know why the book had finally decided to help her, but she wasn't about to lose her opportunity.

Sarah focused all of her attention to the writing on the page, hoping she could decipher the cramped, poorly written characters quickly. She knew the book was capricious and wouldn't help her for long. To Sarah's horror, her fears proved right. She had only made it through the first few sentences, when the words started to fade.

"No!" said Sarah to herself, "I just need a few more minutes."

But, before Sarah could do anything the words had faded almost completely off the page. In their place, appeared a string of musical notes.

"Music?" said Sarah, angrily. "What does that have to do with anything?"

Then, suddenly, it hit her. How could she have been so blind? The book had been trying to tell her all along. It wanted something in exchange for helping her. It wasn't going to give up its secrets without some kind of recompense. The book had started helping her again when Molly was playing the piano. The book must like music, and especially Molly's playing.

"That's it!" said Sarah, excitedly. "I just have to get Molly to play a little longer and I'll have everything I need."

Sarah tripped down the stairs to find Molly returning to the parlor.

"I hope you're going to keep playing," said Sarah.

"I only just started," said Molly. "But I forgot some of my music in the other room."

"You don't mind if I sit in here and read while you play?" asked Sarah, trying to contain her excitement.

"Of course not," said Molly, "if you don't mind a few mistakes."

"Your mistakes sound lovely," said Sarah with a smile. "I wouldn't know there were any mistakes if you didn't tell me."

"Thank you," smiled Molly. "I think you'll be a good audience!"

Molly sat down at the piano and began playing again as Sarah settled down in a chair with the book.

"Now we're going to learn something," said Sarah to herself.

*****

Arthur was beginning to feel very tired. He had followed Jonas Pickering to an old, rundown cottage just outside of Castleton. Jonas was still in the cottage, and it didn't seem as if he was going to leave anytime soon. Arthur had been waiting for some time and he was getting impatient. Why didn't Jonas come out? Arthur knew that Jonas needed to leave the package Mr. Silverstone had given to him at the Four Towers before nightfall. Wasn't it dark out now? Why didn't he come out?

As Arthur continued to wait, he examined the cottage more closely. The structure was in a state of disrepair. It badly needed painting and the front porch looked as if it was about to fall off. The windows were cracked and thickly coated with dirt, making it impossible to see anything inside. Arthur wished that he could look in one of the windows and see what the Jonas was doing. At least it would give him something to do. He was going to fall asleep if Jonas didn't come out soon.

*****

Suddenly, Arthur was awoken by a loud bang. The front door of the house was open and Jonas Pickering was standing on the dilapidated porch. Arthur didn't know how long he had been asleep. It couldn't have been that long. It didn't seem much darker outside. Thank goodness he hadn't missed Jonas leaving the house. That would have been horrible!

"Robbers and thieves, robbers and thieves," said Jonas in a sing song voice. As usual, Jonas was talking very loudly to himself and Arthur could hear him clearly.

"Never trust a fellow robber with your stolen goods," laughed Jonas, gleefully.

"I've got enough stashed away here to get out of this

horrible town for good," he continued, with a grim smile. "And I'm not going to share my riches with anyone, especially not that old fool Silverstone!"

He laughed again and said, "I'll meet the thieves tonight, make my final trade, and be out of here before Silverstone knows what hit him."

Jonas slung a large bag over his back, looked around cautiously, closed the front door of the cottage, and walked down the path that ran in front of his house.

"Off to the Four Towers," he shouted, "to make my fortune!"

Arthur looked after Jonas in wonder. "So he is smuggling stolen goods," Arthur whispered to himself.

Arthur was now certain that Jonas was a thief. But was he also the person behind the disturbances at the Four Towers? Was he really that evil and powerful? Arthur still wasn't sure. But he knew that he had to follow Jonas Pickering to the Four Towers and try to stop him. However, he couldn't do it alone. If Jonas was meeting other criminals, Arthur needed help. He needed to get a message to Daniel and Sarah.

Arthur stepped cautiously onto the rickety front porch. He touched the knob of the front door and turned it slowly. It was unlocked! Arthur was surprised. If Jonas was keeping all of his stolen goods in the house why would he leave the door unlocked? But then it dawned on Arthur. The house was so far out of the way and rundown that no one would ever think to look there for anything.

It took a moment for Arthur to find a light in the cottage. He fumbled around in the dark for a few moments before he was able to find a switch on the wall. He turned the switch on, flooding the room with light. Arthur gasped at the sight that met his eyes. The interior of the cottage was absolutely luxurious, nothing like the seedy, rundown exterior. Jonas Pickering, unbeknownst to everyone in town, was living a life of luxury! Even more incredible, the small room was full of antiques and jewelry, most likely all stolen! Arthur didn't have time to examine things more closely. He saw what he needed almost immediately. Right before him, on a small table, was a telephone. He breathed a sigh of relief and grabbed the phone.

In a few moments Arthur was back outside of the house, rushing towards the Four Towers. Jonas had gotten a good head start. Arthur hoped that he wouldn't be too late.

*****

Sarah was back upstairs in her bedroom. The afternoon had gone wonderfully well, better than she could have hoped. Molly had played beautifully and the book had cooperated. Sarah had made notes of everything that the book had revealed. She was now attempting to decipher what she had written. Sarah sighed, looking at the stack of papers before her. This part might be a bit harder. Even with the music, not everything the book had revealed was clear to her. Nothing was ever as easy as she wanted it to be!

Sarah was also feeling a bit anxious. It was late afternoon, and, although the weather was still nice, the evening promised another storm. Was there something about the coming storm that was making her nervous? Or was she thinking too much about the Four Towers? Sarah didn't know for sure, but she felt a sense of urgency regarding her task. If she could just figure out what was going on she knew she would feel much better.

Sarah laid out five pieces of paper on the table. Each page had a few sentences that she had copied from the book, but she wasn't sure what they all meant.

"Okay," said Sarah to herself, as she read over the papers, "what are you trying to tell me?"

After a few moments of thinking, Sarah started moving the papers around on the table, putting them in different orders.

"They're steps in the process," said Sarah to herself, as she began to understand what the book had been trying to tell her. "These are the steps that must be taken to awaken the stone. I just have to figure out the right order."

110

*Be wary of the Philosopher's Stone!*
*The stone is not what it seems.*
*Fools use the stone to produce gold.*
*But the stone only creates evil, not riches.*

*Step 1: The stone awakens slowly, and only to one of great power.*
*Step 2: Once fully awakened, the stone will test its powers, creating a ring of fire.*
*Step 3: The stone needs a host, a weak mind that it can control.*
*Step 4: The one who woke the stone must provide a host (within three nights after the ring of fire).*
*Step 5: The stone will bind with its host on the first night and start to work evil, unless it is put back to sleep.*

*Beware! Once the stone finds a host, it is almost impossible to put to sleep again.*

*Only one with much power, or the one who woke the stone, can put it back to sleep.*

Sarah gazed at the pages before her in horror. She had been skeptical of the legend of the Four Towers and the evil Philosopher's Stone that Mr. Chen had described. But, now that she had the words of the book before her, she realized it was all true. The stone had certainly changed Edward Montclair for the worse. He must have been the stone's host, although who woke the stone for him was a mystery. His wife, Caroline, had been strong enough to put it to sleep, but only at the cost of her own life.

But now, someone had awoken the stone again. But who? Sarah was at a loss. Could it be Jonas Pickering, as Arthur suspected? Jonas was the only person Sarah had actually seen at the Four Towers. He seemed like such an unlikely candidate though. But if it wasn't Jonas, then who was it? And, even more importantly, who was the host? Sarah's head was whirling. She felt as if the book had provided her with more questions than answers.

However, Sarah knew one thing for certain. She was going to have to try to put the stone back to sleep that very night. She had witnessed the ring of fire exactly (--) days before. The stone was fully awake. And tonight it was supposed to bind with its host.

Sarah didn't know if she was powerful enough to put the stone back to sleep on her own. And, even more importantly, she didn't know if she was strong enough to face the person who had awoken the stone in the first place. But, she knew she couldn't let her fears stop her. She had to try.

Sarah threw a few things into her bag, Mr. Chen's book and the broken locket. She didn't know why, but she felt as if they might offer some protection. At least she wouldn't be facing the dangers of the Four Towers alone. If only Arthur were with her...but that was not to be. There was no time to contact him. She had to get to the Four Towers as quickly as possible.

"I just hope I'm not too late," Sarah said to herself, as she ran downstairs and out of the house.

# CHAPTER XIII
# SACRIFICE

his is just like my last trip to the Four Towers," whispered Sarah to herself.

A thick fog had appeared suddenly, as if from nowhere, obscuring the path and greatly impeding Sarah's progress. Even worse, the storm, which was supposed to start later that evening, had come early. Jagged streaks of lightning and tremendous crashes of thunder were disturbing the quiet country side.

Sarah was feeling increasingly anxious, and not just because of the weather. What she had read in the book was frightening. She knew she had to stop the stone before it found a host. But the book hadn't given her any clues about how to put the stone back to sleep. How was she going to know what to do?

Yet again, Sarah wished that she wasn't going to the Four Towers alone. If only Arthur was with her. With his help, she was sure that they could figure out what to do.

Sarah stumbled and groped her way forward. It felt as if she had been walking forever when she finally reached the clearing where the ruins of the castle stood. As she looked down at the towers, she felt a small sense of relief. There were no strange flashes or flames shooting up from the ruins. In fact, the castle looked almost normal.

"Maybe nothing is going to happen tonight after all," said Sarah to herself hopefully.

However, as soon as Sarah entered the castle grounds, her heart sank. This wasn't normal. All of her senses were immediately heightened and she felt an overwhelming sense of dread. It was bone chillingly cold inside the castle walls. This was not what she had hoped for. Sarah looked down at her ring. It was shining slightly, emitting a dull golden glow into the darkness. She felt her fear rising. Even her ring was warning her away.

Sarah hurried forward, trying to fight the fear that was paralyzing her. She peered through the fog and gloom and could just make out the faint, ghostly outline of the fourth tower. It was there, pulsing eerily in the shadows, waiting for her.

Suddenly, from out of nowhere, Sarah felt a hand clasp her arm. She tried to scream, but could make no sound. Sarah turned sharply, trying to disengage herself from whoever had grabbed her.

"Hey Sarah," said a familiar voice. "Don't worry...it's me."

"Arthur?" said Sarah, relief flooding her voice.

"I didn't mean to scare you," he said.

"What are you doing here?" asked Sarah, wonderingly.

"Following Jonas Pickering," said Arthur. "But I think I got here before him. We were right about him. He is a thief! He's supposed to be exchanging stolen goods here tonight."

"Oh," said Sarah, her head reeling, "as if we don't have enough going on already."

"I know," said Arthur, as he looked towards the fourth tower. "I'd been hoping that you'd imagined the whole thing. This is the first time I've seen it. And it's obviously not my imagination."

"No," said Sarah, with a shiver. "It's horribly real."

"So what are you doing here?" asked Arthur. "I thought we were both supposed to be avoiding the Four Towers."

"We're not very good listeners are we? It's a long story," sighed Sarah. "But basically we need to put the stone back to sleep tonight, before it binds with a host."

"Oh . . . Is that all?" said Arthur, trying to take it all in. "I assume you have a plan," he added hopefully.

"Not really," she said, taking his arm and guiding him towards the ghostly fourth tower. "I still don't know who woke the stone, I don't know who the host is, and I don't know how to put the stone back to sleep."

"Then what are we going to do?" asked Arthur.

"I don't know," said Sarah. "I think we just have to trust that we'll be ready when the time comes."

"I was afraid you'd say that," replied Arthur, with a grimace.

By now, the two were standing directly in front of the shadowy fourth tower. As they watched, the tower gradually took on a more definite shape. Suddenly, there was a bright flash, and the ground beneath the tower shimmered and sank, to be replaced by an open pit. Fire and flames leapt from it, blazing towards the top of the tower. After a few moments, the flames subsided slightly, and a strange glow began to emanate from the pit. Smoke and fog swirled around the tower, making it difficult to see clearly.

Sarah gasped as she looked at the space above the pit. "Can you see it?" she whispered to Arthur.

A rough-hewn stone had appeared, as if from nowhere. It was glowing a dark, angry red, and was suspended directly above the fire in the pit.

Arthur looked at Sarah. "Is that the stone?" he faltered, fear gripping him at the sight.

There was evil and anger emanating from the object before them. They could both feel it.

"Yes," whispered Sarah. "That's what we need to stop."

Suddenly, Sarah and Arthur's attention was distracted from the stone to a figure standing nearby. The smoke from the fire had obscured their surroundings to such an extent that neither of the two had noticed him. But he must have been standing there the entire time.

"Jonas?" said Arthur, uncertainly.

"I don't think that's Jonas," said Sarah, as she stepped forward, trying to get a closer look at the mysterious figure. As

Sarah advanced, the person turned to face her and she gasped in surprise.

"Jordan!" she said, shocked. "What are you doing here? You're not searching for lost sheep again, are you? Now isn't really a good time. You need to get out of here before...."

Sarah's words died as her eyes met those of Jordan. They were cold and lifeless and he had a strange look on his face.

"No," said Jordan, slowly and distinctly. "I didn't lose any sheep. That's not why I'm here."

Sarah and Arthur looked at each other. What was wrong with Jordan? Why was he acting so strangely?

"With all your knowledge, skill and power you still haven't figured it out?" said Jordan. "I even tried to give you a few hints, Sarah," he continued, "once in London and once back at the farm. But you still didn't get it. I've clearly overestimated both of you."

Sarah felt a chill run through her. Jordan! Was he the person who had pursued her in London, and scared her on the path at the farm? And could he really be responsible for awakening the stone? She had never even considered him. From the beginning she had thought he was a little strange, but she was certain that he wasn't evil. Could all of her instincts be wrong?

"Jordan," she said, slowly. "What are you talking about?"

Jordan sighed. "You're not at all what I expected," he said, looking at her with disappointment. "And you're even worse," he continued, with a dismissive glance at Arthur. "I didn't have high expectations for you, but you've dashed what little hope I did have."

Arthur bristled under Jordan's harsh words. "Who are you?" he said angrily. "And what are you doing here?"

"That would take some time to explain," said Jordan. "But at the moment, I think we have more pressing matters to attend to," he added, with a gesture towards the stone.

Sarah's head was awhirl. Jordan was the person who had awoken the stone! It didn't make any sense. Some of the pieces fit, but not all. Sarah shook her head slowly. She couldn't accept it. Jordan couldn't be the villain. He wasn't evil. She knew it!

"You still can't believe that it's me?" said Jordan, mockingly, as if reading Sarah's thoughts.

"I'm not what you think," he continued. "And you're not what I thought you'd be either. Your parents are going to be very disappointed when I bring you back to them."

Sarah gasped and then turned white. What was he talking about? How could Jordan have anything to do with her parents?

"What do you mean?" said Sarah, trying to keep her voice even.

"That's my little surprise for you," laughed Jordan. "It's been so hard to keep it in. Your parents have been so anxious to get you back, after all of these years. Although I really don't know why....you're not what I'd want in a daughter. They thought they finally had you last year with Morlock, but somehow you managed to escape."

"How do you know all of this?" whispered Sarah.

"You could say we're almost siblings," laughed Jordan cruelly. "When I was very young, your parents took me in. I was alone and angry, a blank canvas for them to work their magic upon. And here you see the masterpiece they've created," said Jordan, with a dramatic gesture.

"This can't all be true!" said Arthur, angrily. "You're making things up to throw us off!"

"Oh no I'm not!" snapped Jordan, as he whirled around to face Arthur.

"It's pitiful that you still don't know who you really are," Jordan continued. "I can't believe Alfred hasn't told you. But I guess I can do it for him. If you weren't such a dullard you'd have figured it out by now."

"I don't know what you're talking about," retorted Arthur. "I know exactly who I am."

"No you don't!" Jordan laughed cruely. "You don't know

that you're the long lost son of two wonderful people that Sarah's parents killed back when we were all little children."

Arthur's face paled and he grabbed onto the stone wall behind him for support. "You're lying again!" he said, his shock turning to anger.

"No," said Jordan, suddenly calm, "I'm the first person to tell you the truth. Why do you think you have all of the powers that you do? Why do you think you can be a part of the pathetic little group called the Guardians? It's not because you just happened to be born this way. It's because you were born to two of the most powerful members of the Guardians."

"None of what you're saying is true," gasped Arthur.

"Sarah's parents wanted to kill you as well," continued Jordan, "but, I'll have to finish the job for them."

Arthur's face was red with rage. He rushed towards Jordan, all of his powers concentrated on annihilating his enemy. "I'll make you regret everything you've said!" he shouted.

"Arthur, no!" said Sarah. But it was too late.

Jordan held up his hand and simply pointed towards the stone. As if on command, the stone emitted a beam of light, aimed right at Arthur. The beam hit Arthur squarely in the chest and he fell senseless to the ground.

"What have you done?" said Sarah in horror, rushing towards Arthur.

"I simply magnified and redirected his anger in a more useful direction . . . But I didn't kill him if that's what you're worried about," snapped Jordan. "That's for later. But right now, I need you over here!"

Before Sarah could reach Arthur, she felt herself suddenly pushed to the ground and pulled towards Jordan and the stone. Despite her resistance, there was nothing she could do. Sarah began reciting an incantation to protect herself and Arthur, but with the stone's power to aid him, she knew she was no match for Jordan.

"Aha!" said Jordan, reading her thoughts again. "You can sense the power of the stone. It's a shame that it's been dormant for so long. If only Edward had been able to keep his wife from meddling with the stone. Luckily for us, the stone can't be destroyed. That would have been tragic."

Jordan paused for a moment and turned towards the stone. "Patience," he muttered, before turning back to Sarah. "I hate to admit it, but the stone is a little hard for me to control. But with you here to help, I think we can get the stone to bind with Jonas Pickering."

"Jonas!" said Sarah, in astonishment.

"Don't tell me you didn't realize that Jonas is going to be the host," said Jordan. "Really, you surprise me Sarah! I thought you'd have figured that out, at the very least. He's such a stupid fool, the perfect specimen for a host. I have him stashed back there behind the tower. He's sleeping like a baby. All we have to do is say a few simple spells together and the job will be done."

"I'm not going to help you," said Sarah, defiantly.

"Yes you are," replied Jordan, smoothly. "That's why you're here."

"There's no chance," Sarah replied, glaring at him. "The only thing I'm going to do tonight is put the stone back to sleep, before it's too late."

Jordan laughed and looked at Sarah darkly. "You are going to help me," he said. "You're going to do exactly as I say. Or else your little gang of friends will be destroyed, starting with your precious Arthur."

"You wouldn't dare!" said Sarah, her face turning pale.

"Just try me," said Jordan, with a malicious laugh.

Sarah's mind was racing. It now occurred to Sarah that Jordan was attempting to divide her powers. She realized that she must choose between resisting the stone, and saving Arthur. She had been in difficult situations with Arthur before. She must trust that Arthur is strong enough to survive. Faith and love are the only way to conquer fear and darkness.

Jordan had to be telling the truth about her parents. How else would he know everything that he had told her? But from there, she didn't know what to think. She still couldn't believe that he was truly evil. It was as if there was some other power at work, forcing Jordan to do things that weren't representative of his true self. She had seen him with the animals on the farm, they could sense his goodness. And she could too. So where was this evil coming from?

Suddenly Sarah knew. Her parents...of course! She could see it in Jordan's eyes. He wanted the same things that Sarah had yearned for...love, affection, and care.

"You're not capable of hurting anyone," Sarah said slowly. "You're not the evil person you're pretending to be."

Jordan looked at her for a moment, his eyes flashing. "What do you know about me?" he snapped.

"I know you're lost and alone like I was," said Sarah. "You're trying to find love. But it's not possible. Maybe my parents were capable of love once, but not anymore."

Jordan's face turned red and he looked angry. Then he turned away from Sarah, as if he didn't want her to see his face.

"What do you know about your parents anyway?" he said. "You don't even know them."

"I know enough to know that they aren't going to give you what you need," replied Sarah.

Jordan, with his face still averted from her, said "I don't need anything. I don't know what you're talking about. I'm here to do a job and that's what I'm going to do."

For a brief moment, Sarah felt the force that was dragging her towards Jordan relent ever so slightly, and she was able to claw at the stone floor as she regained some control of her hands.

"You're here to do what my parents ordered you to do," said Sarah. "Not something you want to do."

Jordan whirled around to face Sarah. She could see that his eyes were filled with pain. "Why are you saying all of this? It doesn't matter what I think or how I feel. I don't have a choice in any of this!"

Jordan redoubled his effort to control Sarah, and she found herself once again being dragged back along the floor towards him. With her hands suddenly limp, dragging behind her, she caught site of her ring, and remembered how it had helped her at Westmere.

"Yes you do," said Sarah. "There's always a choice between good and evil. I can help you...just give me a chance...we can do this together..."

Jordan looked away again. "It's too late," he said. "And I'm so tired. I don't have the strength to change now," he whispered.

Sarah rolled onto her back, but was still being dragged along the floor in Jordan's direction. She cupped her palms together, and a bright white light formed an orb between her hands, emanating from her ring. It was love . . . She could feel its power gathering strength.

"Let me help you," said Sarah, gently. "I know we can do this together."

Jordan looked at Sarah intently for a moment. His eyes were still filled with pain. Then he looked towards the stone.

"No," he replied softly. "I started this, I'll finish it."

Sarah stood up. "What are you talking about? We can stop the stone together. Please take this," offering him the quickly growing orb.

"You don't know the stone like I do," said Jordan. "It will destroy us both. I'm not going to let that happen."

Sarah looked at Jordan in alarm. She watched as he walked closer to the pit under the fourth tower. Then suddenly she understood. He was going to sacrifice himself to stop the stone! She couldn't let that happen. She had to stop him.

"Jordan, no!" she said. She tried to run towards him, but she was suddenly stopped by his upraised arm.

Jordan looked towards her. "It would have been nice to get to know you better," he said, regretfully. "We are sort of like step siblings."

"Jordan please!" said Sarah, desperately. "Let me help you.

You don't have to do this!"

"Yes, I do," said Jordan. "I'd like my life to have some meaning."

Sarah understood, then suddenly, she thought of something. She reached into her pocket and grabbed the locket that Mr. Chen had given her.

"At least take this," she said, tossing the locket towards Jordan. "It was Caroline's. It will protect you."

Jordan caught the locket and looked at it curiously. "Thank you," he said softly, grasping it tightly in his hand. As he spoke, he walked to the edge of the pit, turning all of his attention to the stone.

Sarah, in turn, focused all of her attention on the glowing orb that continued to grow in size until it completely engulfed her, Jordan and the Stone. She hoped it would be enough.

Jordan stood completely still for a few moments, gathering his energy, and then looked back at Sarah. "Maybe we'll meet again someday," he said, with a slight smile, "You know, you're the only one who can stop your parents. They're going to come for you. And you need to destroy them."

Sarah nodded numbly.

Without another word, Jordan jumped into the pit, grabbing the stone in his arms as he did so. For a moment, the two were suspended in midair, the stone throbbing and twisting, trying to break away from Jordan's grasp. With a momentous effort, he mastered the stone and held it before him. There was a tremendous explosion of flames, and then everything went dark.

# CHAPTER XIV
# THE AFTERMATH

 arah's eyes fluttered open. It was early evening and the violent storm had ended. There was a fresh, clean smell in the air, as if the storm had washed away the evil of the philosopher's tone.

"Jordan!" whispered Sarah to herself, as she got to her feet. She steadied herself against the castle wall and looked around for him. The area where the fourth tower had been was completely empty. There was no pit, no ghostly shadow of a tower. Nothing to show that there had ever been anything there besides castle ruins. Sarah's heart sank. Jordan was nowhere to be seen.

"Sarah!" said a feeble voice from behind her.

Suddenly Sarah remembered what had happened to Arthur. "Arthur!" she said, rushing to his side. "Are you okay?"

Arthur was standing near where Jordan had stunned him, rubbing his head and looking confused.

"What happened?" he said. "What'd I miss?"

"Everything," replied Sarah.

"It certainly looks that way," said Arthur, glancing towards the ruins of the fourth tower. "I'm sorry I didn't help you," continued Arthur. "But Jordan was so powerful. He took me by surprise."

"He surprised both of us," said Sarah. "But you don't have to apologize for not helping me. Jordan was the one who stopped the stone."

"Where is he?" asked Arthur, looking around.

"I don't know what happened to him," said Sarah. "The last I saw was him leaping into the pit."

"Oh," said Arthur, his eyes widening. "Do you think he's...." Arthur trailed off.

"I don't know," replied Sarah, shakily.

"Only a few minutes ago I thought he was our enemy," said Arthur. "Now he's the one who saved us."

"I know," said Sarah. "And everything he said and the things he knew...."

She paused for a moment, looking at Arthur nervously. "Arthur, I'm so sorry about your parents. I didn't know. I think my uncle might have known, but he didn't tell me. I don't know how you're going to think of me after this. I'm so sorry..."

Arthur looked at Sarah and took her hand, holding it tightly. "Sarah, what happened had nothing to do with you. Nothing can change our friendship, you have to know that."

Sarah nodded gratefully.

"It never occurred to me that my parents were Guardians," said Arthur, slowly. "I've been trying to figure out what I should do with my life. Knowing who my parents were changes everything."

"It's funny," continued Arthur, thoughtfully. "Even though I know that my parents are gone, I feel like I've gained something, not like I've lost something."

Sarah looked at Arthur and smiled. "I'm so glad," she said.

Just then, Sarah and Arthur heard a low moaning sound coming from the corner of the wall behind them.

"What is that?" said Sarah.

She and Arthur walked towards the direction from which the sounds were coming.

"Oh no!" said Arthur, as they turned the corner of the castle wall. "We completely forgot about poor Jonas!"

"Do you think he's okay?" asked Sarah, looking curiously at the sleeping figure of Jonas Pickering.

"I'm sure he will be eventually," said Arthur. "He doesn't look any worse than normal. In fact, I think he looks very peaceful."

"It's nice to have a quiet Jonas for a change," said Sarah, with a smile.

"And that reminds me!" said Arthur, "I called Daniel right before I came here. I told him what Jonas was up to, and he said he'd contact the police. They should be here any minute!"

"Then we need to get our story straight," said Sarah. "Luckily there isn't any trace of the philosopher's stone or the fourth tower, but we still need to be able to explain why we're here."

"Right," said Arthur, thinking quickly. "We can keep close to the truth. We were suspicious of Jonas. We found out what he was up to and we followed him here to try to stop him. Sound good?"

"It'll have to do," said Sarah. "I think we have company."

Just then, there was a loud noise of cars and sirens. In a moment, Sarah and Arthur were surrounded by the local police force, Molly, Daniel, and Molly's aunt and uncle.

"We were so worried about you!" said Molly, giving Sarah a hug. "When Daniel told us that you were out here following Jonas and that he was a criminal we didn't know what to think. I'm so glad you're both okay!"

"We're fine," said Arthur. "By the time we got here, Jonas was fast asleep."

"But you shouldn't have come out here at all!" said Caroline, looking at the two in concern. "We were both worried sick! To be out in the storm was unthinkable! But to be out here when thieves and criminals are roaming about...it's terrible!"

Why didn't you tell us?" asked Jacob. "We could have helped."

"There wasn't any time," said Arthur. "We weren't sure that Jonas was really a thief until this afternoon. I barely had time to call Daniel. I was lucky that Jonas had a working phone in his cottage."

"I think Jonas had just about every luxury a person could want in that rundown cottage of his," said one of the policemen.

"It surprised me," said Arthur. "It looks so terrible from the outside!"

The policeman nodded in agreement. "We sent a few of the other constables over to the cottage as a precaution, just in case Jonas went back there. They were certainly shocked when they saw the inside! But it was lucky we had the place covered. We caught the other thieves that Jonas was supposed to meet here. They had decided to double cross him and rob his cottage while he was waiting here for them.

"No honor among thieves," said Arthur.

"You were just lucky those cutthroats didn't come here to meet Jonas!" said Caroline. "I can't even bring myself to imagine what might have happened."

"We're both okay," said Sarah, reassuringly. "And we're sorry we didn't tell you. It just all happened so fast."

"We have to thank you for figuring things out and putting yourselves in danger," said the policemen. "Jonas Pickering and the other thieves would have gotten away if it wasn't for you."

"You need to thank Daniel," said Arthur, pointing towards his friend. "He's the one who suspected that something was wrong in the first place."

"Well, regardless," said the policeman, "We appreciate everything that all of you did."

"And now, if you don't mind, could a few of you help us out?" asked the policeman. "We need to get Jonas down to the car."

Daniel, Arthur, and Jacob joined the policemen as they walked over to the slumbering figure of Jonas, leaving Molly, Sarah, and Caroline alone. They were standing near the place where the Fourth Tower should have been, gazing at the ruins silently.

Molly looked at Sarah curiously. "I have a feeling that

there's more to the story than what you've told us."

Sarah tried her best to look as if she didn't know what Molly was talking about. "I don't know what you mean," she answered.

Molly rolled her eyes. "Just like at Westmere," she said. "I hope you know I don't believe you. But I'm not going to pry. I'll let you have your secrets."

Caroline looked around at the ruins and then at Sarah. "It does feel different here. It's as if something bad has been put to rest. I suppose that means that there aren't going to be any more strange disturbances at the Four Towers."

Sarah shook her head slowly. "No," she replied. "I think that's all over for now."

"Well for that I thank you," said Caroline. "This place is special to so many of us. It's good to know that the castle is finally at peace."

She paused for a moment and then said, "We should probably join the others. It looks like they're ready to go."

"I'll just be a minute," said Sarah. "I want to take one last look."

"Of course," said Caroline, taking Molly by the arm. "We'll wait for you."

Sarah stood by herself for a few more moments, looking at the place where the fourth tower had been.

"Good bye Jordan," she whispered softly, as she walked away from the ruins.

# CHAPTER XV
# RESOLUTION

ne day had passed since the arrest and capture of Jonas Pickering. All of the excitement at the Four Towers had been resolved just in time. The next day, everyone was going their separate ways. The farewell celebration was already underway, with Eustace busily preparing his breakfast feast in the farmhouse kitchen.

Most of the guests had already arrived. Arthur and Daniel had come over from Castleton together, bringing a very despondent Mrs. Bannerbee with them. She didn't know what she was going to do without her two young friends. They had become a part of the family. Margaret, Eustace, and Tad had arrived much earlier. Eustace needed extra time to prepare his legendary pastry breakfast buffet.

The sounds coming from the kitchen were alarming, but also a mark that things were back to normal. As always, Eustace's meal preparation involved making a giant mess and fighting with his sister Margaret.

"Why can't you be more helpful?" moaned Eustace, looking mournfully at a burnt batch of scones. "All you had to do was take these out of the oven when the timer beeped. How difficult is that?"

Margaret scowled. "Eustace, you know I despise cooking and baking! Why can't you get someone else to help you? Anyway, it's not my fault your stupid scones are burnt. How can I listen for timers beeping when I'm planning important business deals?"

Eustace looked around. "I don't see any business people! We're in a kitchen!"

"I'm always working in my head," said Margaret. "It's what smart, successful people do. You wouldn't know how that feels. Anyway, I think you have enough scones already. You've already made about six trays."

"It's always good to have extra," said Eustace. "That's what smart, successful people do!" he muttered, under his breath.

"What was that?" said Margaret, looking at her brother suspiciously.

"Nothing," said Eustace, with an impish grin.

"Hey, do you think you could watch this pan for a minute while I get some sugar?" he asked, looking at Margaret doubtfully.

"I guess," said Margaret, reluctantly. "But it's the last thing I'm going to do for you. Then I'm leaving to join the others."

Eustace rummaged around on the counter, trying to find the sugar in the mess he had made. "Here we are," he said finally, walking back to the stove and taking the spoon from Margaret.

He stirred the pot a few times, looking at its contents anxiously. "Phew, you didn't ruin it," he said.

Margaret looked at the contents of the pan she had been stirring and then looked at Eustace. "Is this chocolate?" she asked.

"Of course, isn't it obvious?" said Eustace. "It's for the chocolate cream puffs. Luckily you weren't in charge of those and they didn't get ruined."

Margaret looked at the chocolate and then said quickly, "Do you think we could make a cream puff with extra chocolate sauce?"

"Why?" said Eustace. "You hate chocolate."

"It's not for me," she said, shortly.

"Well if it's not for you, then who's it for?" demanded Eustace. "You never do anything for anyone else."

"I'd prefer not to say," said Margaret, angrily.

Eustace looked at her for a moment, his face showing surprise. "Is it for Tad?!" he asked, incredulously. "I think you like him!" he crowed.

Margaret flushed, her face turning an angry red. "Never mind," she snapped. "Forget I said anything!"

Eustace looked at her red face, and then began laughing gleefully. "You have a crush on Tad! Who should I tell first?"

Margaret scowled and looked away. She shouldn't have said anything to Eustace. Of course he would turn it into a joke and tell everyone! She looked around the kitchen, hoping she could find something to hurl at her brother. It wouldn't solve the problem, but at least it would make her feel better.

Luckily for Eustace, Molly entered the kitchen at that moment.

"What can I help with?" she asked. "Did I interrupt something?" she added, looking from one sibling to the other.

"Actually you did," said Eustace eagerly. "Margaret was just telling me about her undying love for..."

Margaret elbowed Eustace roughly out of her way to grab a large tray of pastries. "Here, she said, handing the tray to Molly. "You can bring these out to the dining room."

"Sure," said Molly, taking the tray from Margaret and leaving the kitchen.

"Ow," said Eustace, rubbing his arm. "What'd you do that for?"

"You know why I did it," said Margaret, menacingly. "And you better keep your mouth shut or there'll be more where that came from."

"I don't care," said Eustace. "You do that stuff to me all the time anyway!"

Margaret glared at her brother and was silent. Then, after a moment she said, "If you keep your mouth shut, I'll help you with Molly."

Eustace looked at Margaret, his eyes widening. If he had Margaret on his side in his quest to win Molly, he was sure to prevail. "You would do that?" he asked.

"Yes, said Margaret. "As long as you stay out of my business and keep quiet about Tad."

"It's a deal," said Eustace, excitedly. As he spoke, he walked over to the stove where the chocolate sauce was still gently simmering. He took a large cream puff and smothered it in melted chocolate.

"Take this," he said. "You can put it at Tad's place."

Margaret smiled at him and almost looked affectionate. "Thank you," she said. "And don't worry, we'll win Molly over. Pritchards always get what they want!"

*****

A few minutes later, everyone was gathered around the large dining room table. All of the food was ready and the celebration was about to begin. Eustace entered the room carrying his last tray of pastries.

"I'm very impressed," said Caroline, admiring all of the delicious food. "You certainly have a talent."

Eustace beamed. "Thank you," he said. "I'm glad some people appreciate my abilities," he added, glaring at Margaret.

"Where's Uncle Jacob?" asked Molly. "I thought he said he was just running out to the barn. Shouldn't he be back by now?"

As if on cue, Molly's uncle walked into the room, looking a bit mysterious.

"There you are!" said Molly. "We were just about to start without you!"

"Sorry I'm late," said Jacob. "But I have a special guest who wanted to join us."

With that Jacob moved aside and Alfred emerged from behind him.

"Uncle Alfred!" said Sarah in surprise. "I didn't know you were going to be here!"

"I didn't either, said Alfred. "I wasn't supposed to get to

London until tomorrow afternoon. But, things changed and here I am. We thought it would be nice if we could surprise everyone."

Sarah went over to his side and hugged him. "I'm so glad," she said. "We have a lot to tell you."

"Yes," said Alfred, a bit gravely. "Jacob was telling me some of what happened on our ride over from Castleton. It sounds like you were both in danger."

"We're okay," said Arthur. "We can tell you all about it later. Right now, I think we need to start eating. I don't know about any of you, but I'm starving."

"You're always starving," groaned Sarah.

"I'm starving too," said Eustace, grabbing a huge croissant from one of the trays.

"I don't see how that's possible," said Margaret, "You ate half of the food in the kitchen before we could get it out here."

"That's why I always make extra," said Eustace, around bites of his food.

\*\*\*\*\*

"So what are all of your plans for the coming year?" asked Jacob, looking around the crowded table. He was buttering his third croissant of the meal and looking very pleased with his bountiful breakfast.

"We know Molly's going to be studying music in New York, but we don't know about the rest of you," said Caroline.

Margaret spoke up first, as she always did. "I'll be going to school in New York City and working at one of the Pritchard firms."

"Won't that keep you very busy?" asked Caroline.

"I like to be busy," she replied. "Plus, they definitely need someone in New York to look after the Pritchard interests. And of course, I'm the perfect person for that."

"What about you Tad?" asked Jacob, curiously. "I'd love to keep you here on the farm with me!"

Tad smiled. "Thank you," he said. "I wish I could stay longer, but I just found out I have a job waiting for me at the Pritchard firm in New York City too. I'll be moving there in the next few weeks."

Eustace, who was in the midst of ingesting a large chocolate eclair, breathed in sharply and began coughing violently.

"Are you alright?" asked Caroline in concern.

"Yes," gasped Eustace. "I was just shocked that...."

"You what?" interrupted Margaret sharply, with a significant glance at Molly.

Eustace glanced from Margaret to Molly and took a deep breath. "Nothing," he said. "I just swallowed wrong, that's all."

"Well that sounds wonderful," smiled Caroline at Tad. "I'm sure you'll love New York City, and you already have a friend there in Margaret, so that makes it even nicer for both of you."

Eustace made a snorting sound, which was instantly silenced by another warning glance from Margaret.

What about you and Arthur, Sarah?" asked Jacob. "Alfred mentioned that you might be traveling with him for a little while."

"I don't think we've figured everything out yet," said Sarah, "but that's the plan right now."

"That sounds nice," said Caroline. "Just make sure that you keep these two safe and out of trouble, Alfred," she added.

"Of course," smiled Alfred. "I think they've had enough excitement for some time. Our travels should be much more peaceful."

"And what about you Daniel?" asked Jacob. "Molly said something about California."

"That's right," he answered. "I just found out I was accepted to an engineering school in California."

"That's wonderful!" said Jacob. "You must be very excited."

"I am," said Daniel. "I've wanted to be an engineer since I was a kid."

"Won't that be hard on you and Molly since she's going to

be on the other side of the country?" asked Jacob, jokingly. "It's going to be a long distance romance."

"Actually," said Molly, exchanging a conspiratorial glance with Daniel, "we have a confession to make."

"You're not getting married are you?" asked Jacob, jokingly.

"No," laughed Molly, "but Daniel and I aren't actually dating either."

"What!?" said Jacob and Caroline together, shocked. Eustace let out a strangled yelp and then was silent.

"We haven't been dating since early this summer," said Molly. "We're still best friends and always will be, but we aren't boyfriend and girlfriend."

"I don't understand. Why did you tell us you were dating?" asked Caroline.

"It's been our deep dark secret," said Molly.

"We didn't tell anyone the truth, not even our friends," added Daniel.

"I was afraid that if Uncle Jacob knew that I didn't have a boyfriend he'd try to set me up with one of the neighbors. I didn't want to be harassed during my entire visit."

"Oh," said Caroline, understandingly. "You have a point. Your uncle can be quite the matchmaker when he gets the chance."

Jacob looked annoyed for a moment and then he laughed. "Caroline's probably right. I would have bothered you all summer. You had me completely fooled though."

Molly and Daniel exchanged a smile.

"We still like each other," said Molly, "but it's more like brother and sister."

"I can understand that," said Margaret, looking at Eustace, "you know how much I adore Eustace."

Eustace looked at Margaret uncertainly. "What?" he said.

"You know," said Margaret, "all of that sibling love that we have. I may not always show it, but I'm glad you're my brother. And, because of that, I've arranged a little surprise for you. I might as well tell everyone now.

Eustace looked nervous. "I don't like surprises," he said.

"You'll like this one," said Margaret. "I know you were planning on going back to Westmere in the fall for your last year of school, but I miss you when we're apart. If you'd like, I can arrange for you to attend a pastry school in New York instead.

Eustace gasped. "Are you serious?" he said.

"Of course," said Margaret. "I never joke about anything."

"I'd like that a lot," said Eustace, hardly daring to look at Molly.

"We'll all have lots of time to spend together," said Margaret. "You, me, Molly, and Tad...won't that be wonderful?"

Molly looked at Margaret and smiled. "I think everyone gets nervous when you say things like that Margaret," she said. "They seem so unlike you. But I'll be happy to have friends close by."

"Me too," said Eustace, with a happy smile.

*****

A few hours later the meal was over. It had been a great success. Eustace had outdone himself yet again and everyone was completely stuffed with pastries.

Sarah was about to join everyone in the kitchen to help with the clean up when Jacob took her aside. "I have something to give you," he said, looking a little confused.

"What is it?" asked Sarah, smiling at him.

"It's something from Jordan," he said, "but it doesn't really make sense to me. Maybe it will make sense to you."

Sarah's face turned pale and she looked up at him nervously.

"I don't know if anyone's noticed," continued Jacob, "but Jordan's gone. He had to leave, some sort of family emergency, from what he says in his letter."

Sarah felt her mind reeling. Was it possible? Could Jordan still be alive?

"Do you know when he left the letter?" Sarah asked.

"I'm not sure," said Jacob. "But I think it was after everything that happened at the Four Towers. I'm assuming he left it for me early this morning, but I can't say for sure. I may not have noticed it last night because of all the excitement."

Sarah nodded, trying not to get her hopes up.

"He mentions you in the letter," said Jacob, looking at Sarah curiously.

"He does?" said Sarah, trying to keep her voice steady. "We didn't really talk much while he was here, but he seemed nice, just a little quiet."

"He was an incredibly good person," said Jacob thoughtfully. "He was the best worker I've ever had here. But it's more than that. There was something else about him too...something special."

"What did he say in the letter?" asked Sarah, anxiously.

"Oh yes," said Jacob, recollecting. "Why don't I just let you read it yourself?" he said. "I promised Caroline I'd help clean up the mess Eustace made in the kitchen."

"And this is for you," added Jacob, handing her a small object wrapped in paper. "It was left with the letter."

"Thanks," she said, taking the object from Jacob mechanically, barely even looking at it. All she could think about was the letter. As soon as Jacob was gone, Sarah walked over to a quiet corner of the room. She took a deep breath and opened the letter.

Dear Jacob,

I know I was supposed to stay for another week. But some family problems have come up and I have to leave now. I'm sorry. I enjoyed working with you and I appreciate your kindness.

PS Please return this to Sarah and thank her.

Sarah looked at the small, paper wrapped object in her hand. Could it be what she thought it was? She did her best to pull the paper off, but her hands were shaking. Finally, after what seemed like an eternity, she was able to remove the object from its wrappings. In her hand, she held the broken locket which she had given to Jordan before he jumped into the pit with the philosopher's stone.

He was still alive! He had to be.

*****

Sarah was still trying to make sense of Jordan's letter when she was approached by Arthur and Alfred.

"I guess we need to talk," said Sarah, trying to pull her mind back to the present and away from thoughts of Jordan.

"I told everyone we were going to show Alfred around the farm," said Arthur. "I thought it would be easier for us to talk outside."

The three walked towards the door, emerging into a beautiful summer afternoon.

"It's lovely out here," said Alfred, appreciatively. "It's not often that I get out to the countryside. I'm glad the two of you were able to spend some time here, although it wasn't as peaceful as planned."

"No," said Arthur ruefully. "I was really hoping for a vacation."

"Guardians are never on vacation," replied Alfred seriously.

"I know," laughed Arthur. "Sarah keeps telling me that. I think it's been the theme of this entire trip."

"Do you want us to tell you what happened last night?" asked Sarah.

"I already know most of it," said Alfred. "I paid a visit to my old friend Mr. Chen in town early this morning."

"Oh," said Sarah. "Then you probably know more than we do, and we were actually there!"

"Mr. Chen is very well informed about most things," said Alfred, with a smile.

"We noticed," smiled Sarah.

"I'm just glad that you're both unharmed," said Alfred, a bit more gravely. "All of this was very unexpected. The Guardians were aware of the history surrounding the Fourth Tower, but nothing of much concern has happened there in a very long time. I think what worries me most is the appearance of this Jordan...."

Alfred trailed off.

"I had a bad feeling about him from the beginning," said Arthur.

"No," said Sarah. "Please don't say that. He isn't evil, I know it."

"You speak as if he were still with us," said Alfred. "From what Mr. Chen told me it sounded like he perished with the stone."

"I think he might have survived," said Sarah, handing Alfred the letter and the locket.

"He had to have written this letter after everything that happened," she said. "And he returned the locket! I threw it to him as protection when he went into the pit. It was the only thing he would do to let me help him."

"Are you sure all of this is true, Sarah?" asked Alfred, looking at her kindly. "If Jordan was really sent by your parents then he might be as devious as they are. Don't you think it's possible that he's trying to gain your trust so that in the future he could do something to harm you?"

Sarah shook her head vehemently. "No," she said firmly. "I know that he's good. He's hurt and suffering, but he's not like my parents. I know he's not going back to them."

"What do you think Arthur?" asked Alfred. "You were there too. What were your impressions of Jordan?"

Arthur turned red and looked away for a moment.

"Actually," he said, "Jordan overpowered me at the very beginning. I didn't see anything that happened. I got angry after he told me about my parents...." Arthur faltered, unsure of how to proceed.

"Ahhh," said Aflred. "I owe you an apology for that. I should have told you much sooner. But I didn't think you were ready. That's the only reason I held off for so long."

"I don't think I was ready," said Arthur. "I let my anger take control and Jordan was able to overwhelm me. If I hadn't reacted the way I did, I might have been able to help Sarah."

"We all have to learn one way or the other," said Alfred. "The way to goodness is sometimes marred by evil. We try to keep to the right path as much as we can."

"I know," said Arthur. "I wish I hadn't acted the way that I did, but I am glad that Jordan told me. I don't know if I would have believed anyone else. It's good to know who my parents really were."

"I'm glad you can see it that way," said Alfred gently. "I'm sure there's some pain mixed in there too."

"I do feel loss," said Arthur, "but I think I've gained something too, if that makes any sense."

"I think we can all understand that sentiment," said Alfred.

Arthur was silent for a moment and then said, "How long have you known about my parents?"

"From almost the very first day," said Alfred, with a small smile. "You reminded me of your father and I suspected right away. But all of us thought that you were lost long ago. We didn't think it was possible that you could have survived. I had to find out more before I told you the truth."

"And what did you find?" asked Arthur, curiously.

"That's a much longer story for another day," said Alfred. "Right now, we need to talk about your plans for the future. Part of the reason I wanted you both to take this vacation was so that you would have time to think. I was hoping it would be a little more relaxing for you both, but perhaps it's for the best. Sometimes difficulties help us solidify our plans."

Arthur spoke up first. "I'd like to take more time meeting other Guardians, especially those who knew my parents. The time we spent together this summer traveling and meeting others in the group was amazing. I learned so much and I know there's so much more to learn."

Alfred smiled. "I already have a travel plan in mind for

you. Also, there's someone I'd like you to meet, someone who helped you long ago."

Arthur's eyes opened wider. "You mean the person who saved me?"

"Yes," said Alfred. "I thought it would be good for you to spend some time with him."

Arthur nodded. "I couldn't agree more," he said.

"And you Sarah?" asked Alfred, looking kindly at this niece.

Sarah looked at her uncle and sighed. "I wish I felt the same as Arthur," she said. "But I don't think I can do much more traveling right now. I've spent my whole life with Guardians, sent from one to the next, hiding so that my parents wouldn't discover me. I'm so tired of running and fighting. I don't know how to say this, but I think I need some time away."

"I was hoping you would say that," he said. "I was going to tell you the same thing."

Sarah felt her eyes fill with tears. She didn't think that her uncle would understand. Yet here he was, completely in agreement with her.

"Thank you," she said, looking at him gratefully.

"There's a small school that I know of," continued Alfred. "It's always been very friendly to our group. I'd like you to continue your education there. Guardians always go to college, and I don't want you or Arthur to be any different. Part of the school is devoted to botany. I know you would enjoy learning about plants and flowers. And I think it would be a nice change of pace."

Sarah smiled and nodded at her uncle. "It sounds perfect," she said. "But I don't want you to think that I'm going to let myself get rusty. I don't want to stay away forever. I just need a little break."

"I know," said Alfred. "Don't worry...you can't get off the hook that easily. But I do want you to have some time to rest. And, while you're doing that, you can continue your education. When you're ready to come back, you'll know."

Sarah and Arthur looked at each other. How had Alfred known everything that was in their hearts and minds?

"I think the only thing that bothers me about all of this," said Arthur, "is that we're going to be away from each other for so long. The two of you feel like family."

"It won't be that long," said Alfred. "I'll be traveling with you for a little while, Arthur. And, your travels include the place where Sarah will be studying."

"We won't have a chance to miss each other," smiled Sarah.

"We're always together in spirit anyway," said Alfred, "no matter where we are. Guardians are always connected."

"And now we should probably be getting back," he continued. "Everyone is going to be wondering what happened to us."

"I know," said Arthur. "Luckily they're probably done with the cleanup by now. I think we stayed away just long enough."

"I wonder when we'll all be together like this again," said Sarah, musingly. "It's been nice having all of our friends here."

"It might be sooner than you think," said Alfred. "You never know what the future holds."

# THE END?

# STARGAZER BOOKS

Stargazer Books is a small publishing house with big dreams . . . to find out more please visit

www.stargazerbooks.com

If you enjoyed this book and would like to help us "spread the words" . . . please leave a review on

or LIKE and SHARE on

Look for other books by author Kerry Marie Sloan

## The Fountain of Death
(A Perfectly Silly Mystery)

Young Adult Fiction
for ages 11 and up

## The Book of Westmere
First in The Guardian Series

Young Adult Fiction
for ages 11 and up

## ATNAS
The South Pole Elf

Children's Book
Please read to your child

Look for upcoming books by author Kerry Marie Sloan

# Witches Academy

The Guardian Series by author Kerry Marie Sloan

# The Book of Westmere
# The Four Towers

www.ingramcontent.com/pod-product-compliance
Lightning Source LLC
Chambersburg PA
CBHW060422260626
47161CB00005B/1747